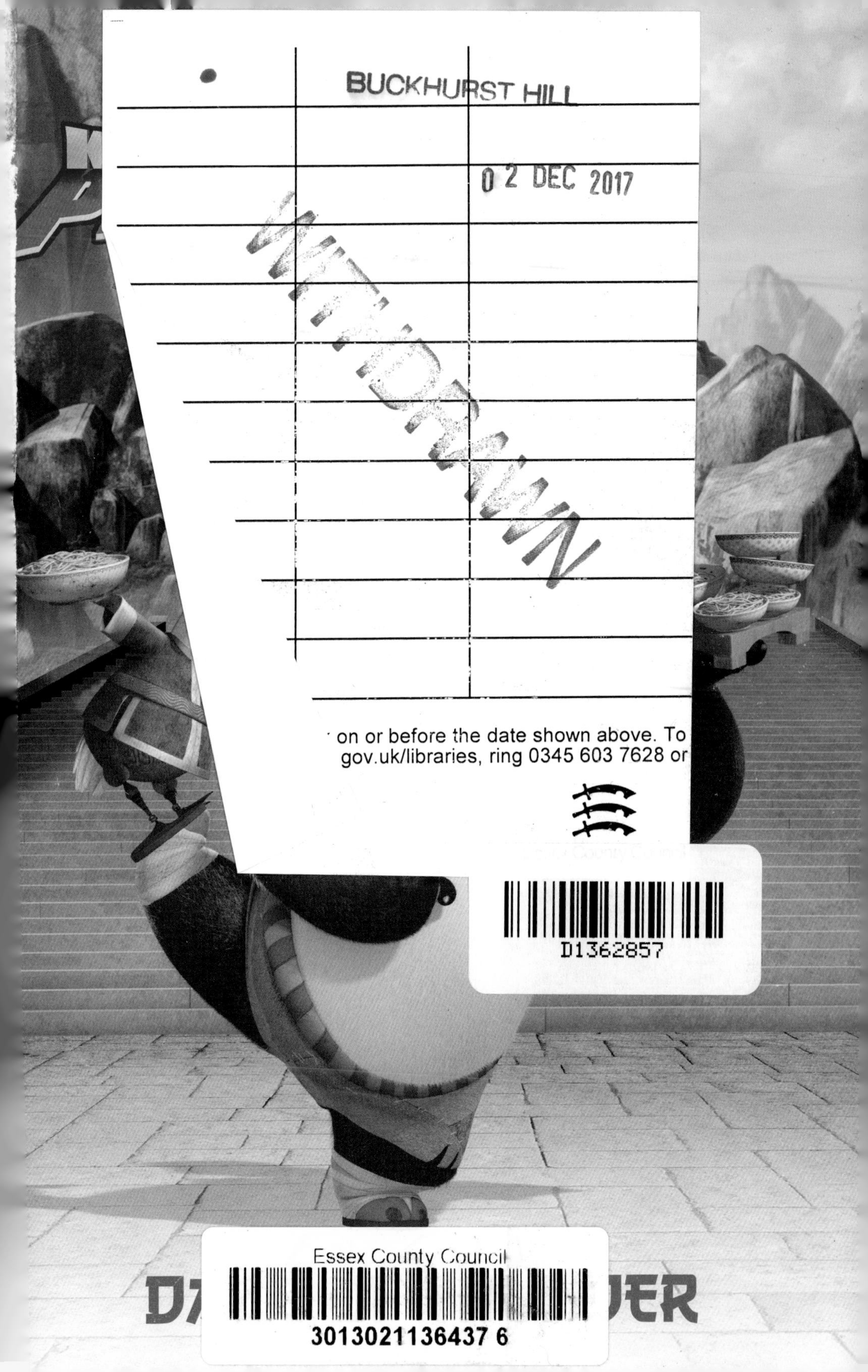

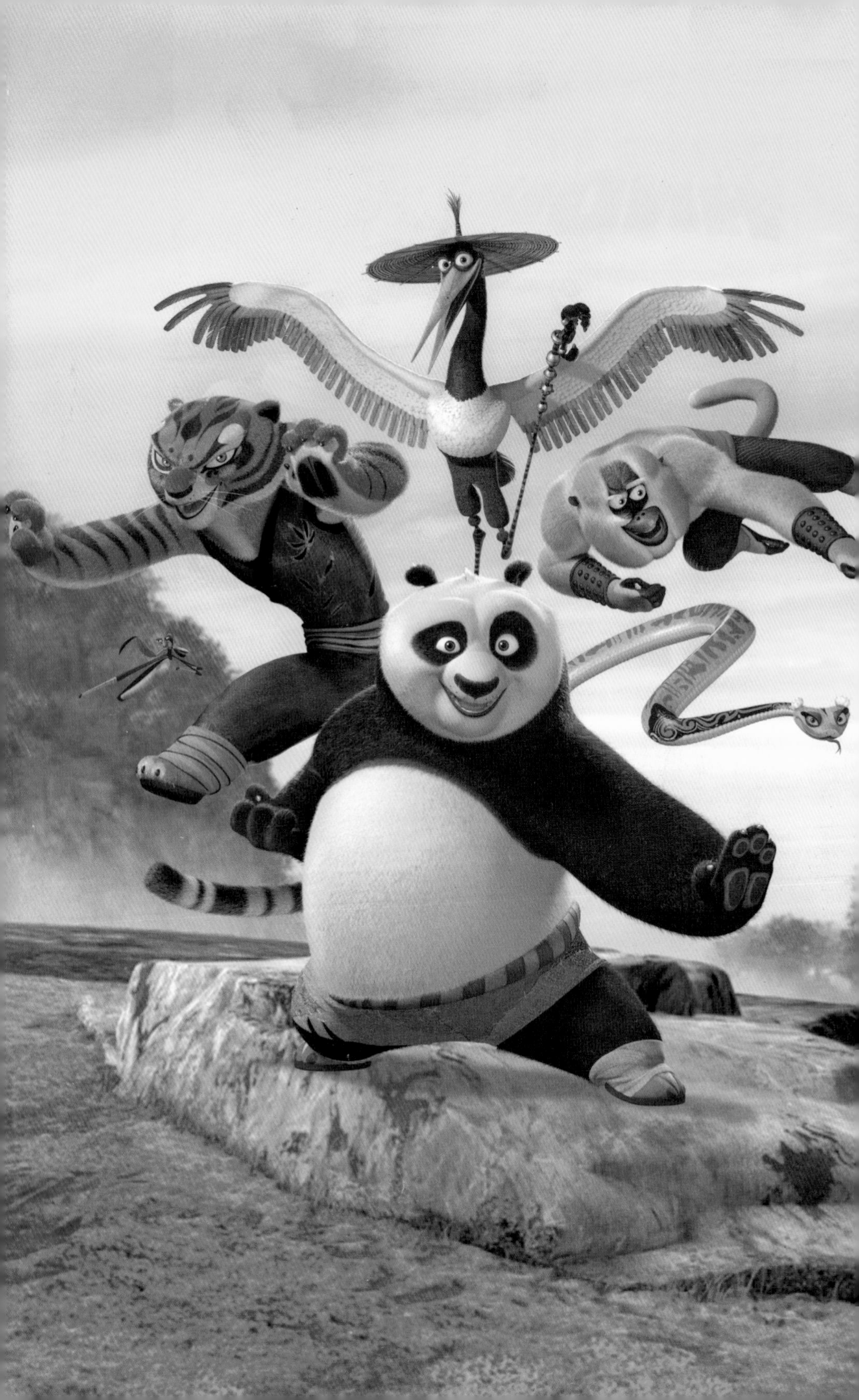

KUNG FU PANDA

VOLUME 1

DAZE OF THUNDER

SCRIPT
Simon Furman

ART
Zak Simmonds-Hurn

LETTERING
Jim Campbell

COLORS
Tracy Bailey

DIVIDE AND CONQUER

SCRIPT
Simon Furman

ART
Lucas Ferreyra

LETTERING
Jim Campbell

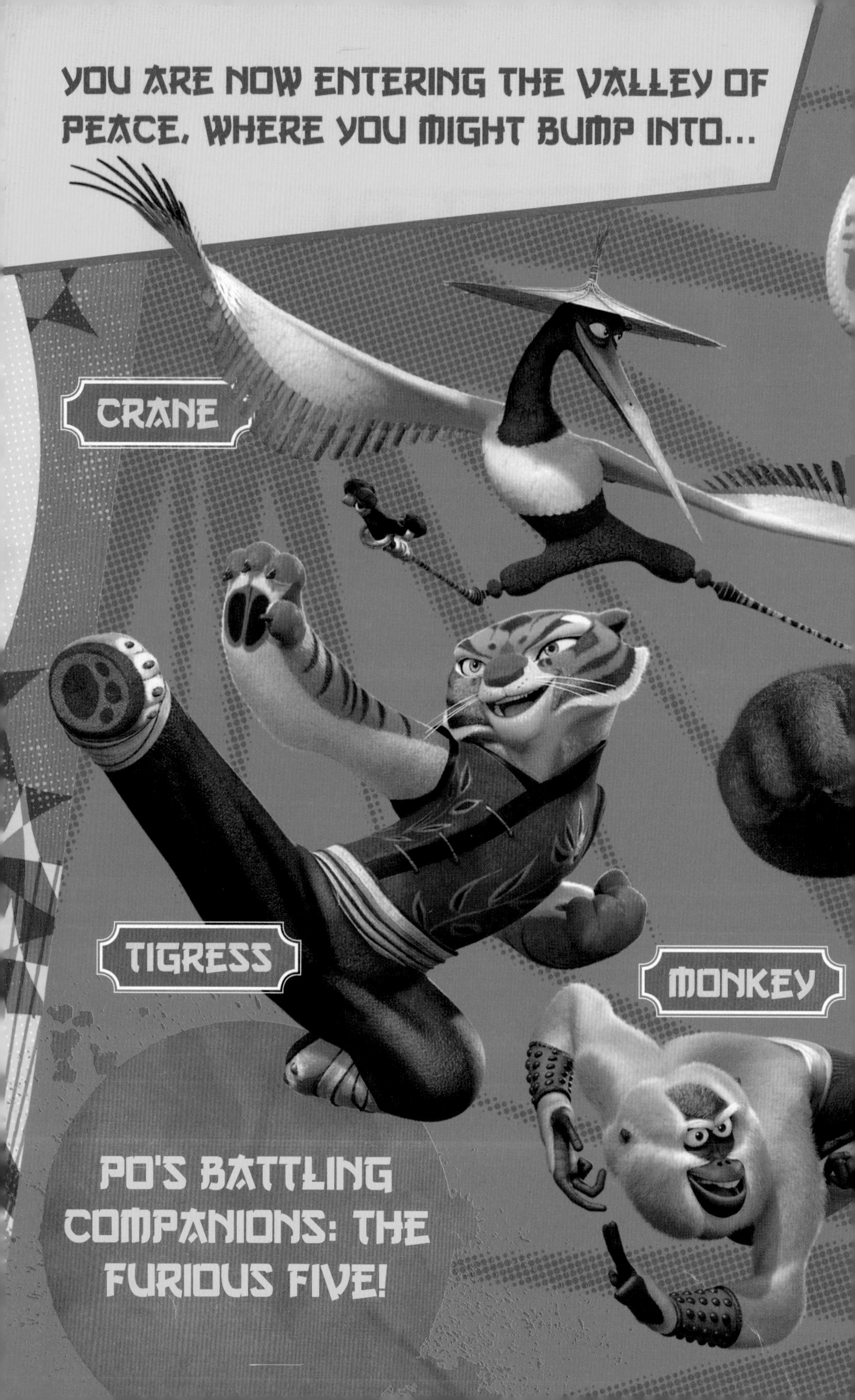
YOU ARE NOW ENTERING THE VALLEY OF PEACE, WHERE YOU MIGHT BUMP INTO...
CRANE
TIGRESS
MONKEY
PO'S BATTLING COMPANIONS: THE FURIOUS FIVE!

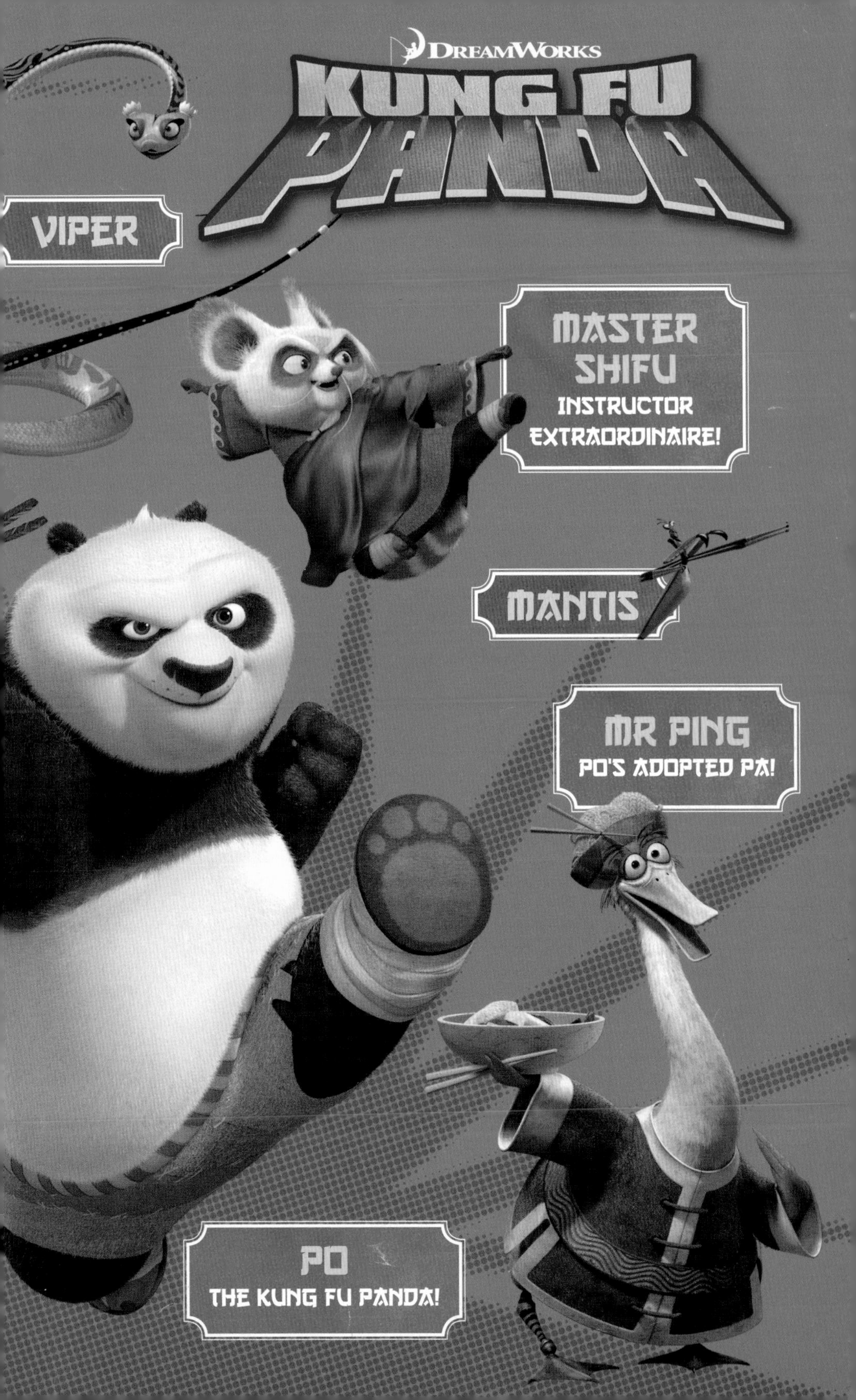
DreamWorks
KUNG FU PANDA
VIPER
MASTER SHIFU
INSTRUCTOR EXTRAORDINAIRE!
MANTIS
MR PING
PO'S ADOPTED PA!
PO
THE KUNG FU PANDA!

TITAN COMICS

SENIOR EDITOR
Martin Eden

ASSISTANT EDITOR
Louisa Owen

PRODUCTION MANAGER
Obi Onuora

PRODUCTION SUPERVISORS
Maria James
Jackie Flook

PRODUCTION ASSISTANT
Peter James

STUDIO MANAGER
Selina Juneja

SENIOR SALES MANAGER
Steve Tothill

MARKETING MANAGER
Ricky Claydon

PUBLISHING MANAGER
Darryl Tothill

PUBLISHING DIRECTOR
Chris Teather

OPERATIONS DIRECTOR
Leigh Baulch

EXECUTIVE DIRECTOR
Vivian Cheung

PUBLISHER
Nick Landau

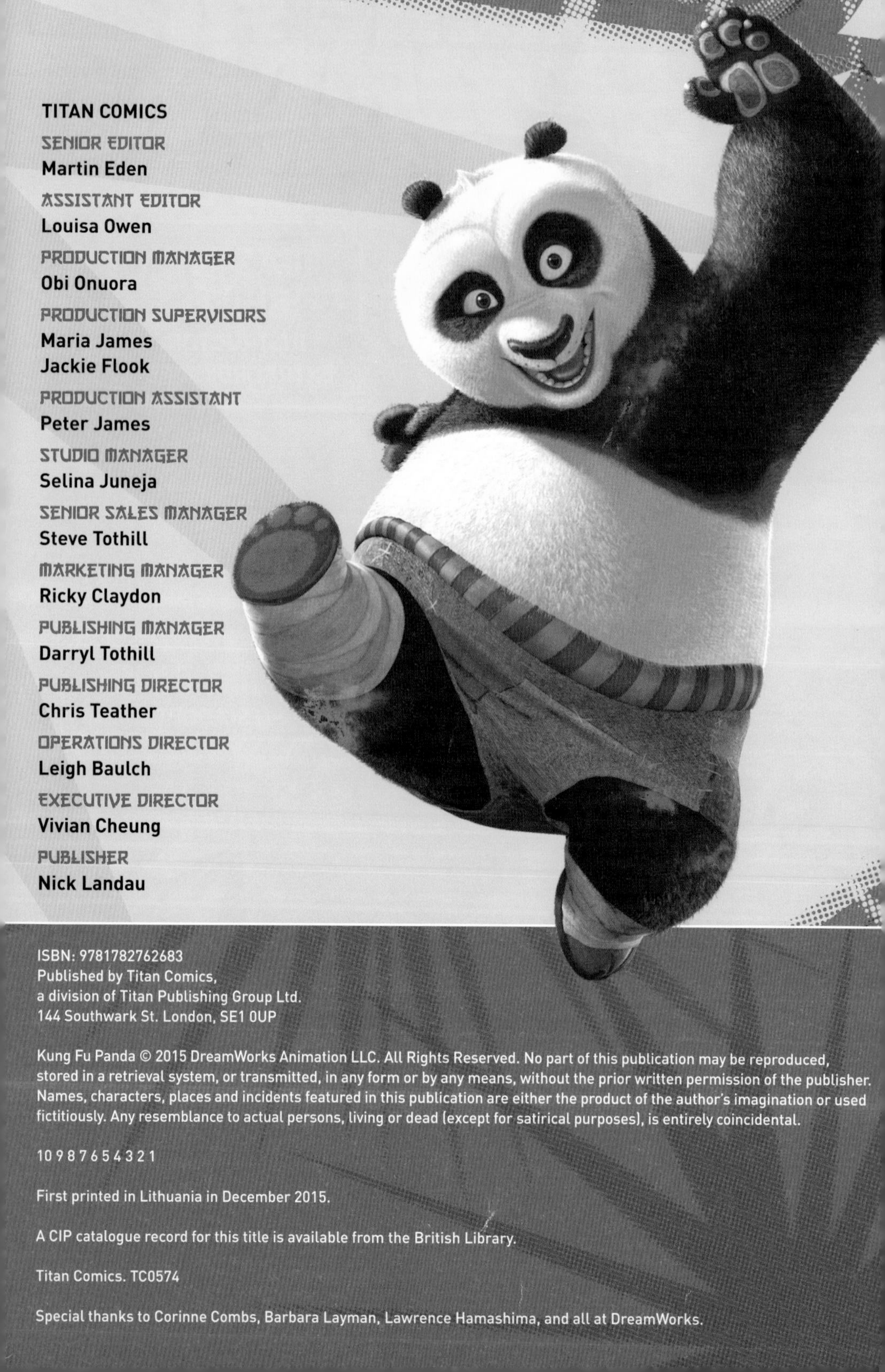

ISBN: 9781782762683
Published by Titan Comics,
a division of Titan Publishing Group Ltd.
144 Southwark St. London, SE1 0UP

10 9 8 7 6 5 4 3 2 1

First printed in Lithuania in December 2015.

A CIP catalogue record for this title is available from the British Library.

Titan Comics. TC0574

Special thanks to Corinne Combs, Barbara Layman, Lawrence Hamashima, and all at DreamWorks.

DAZE OF THUNDER

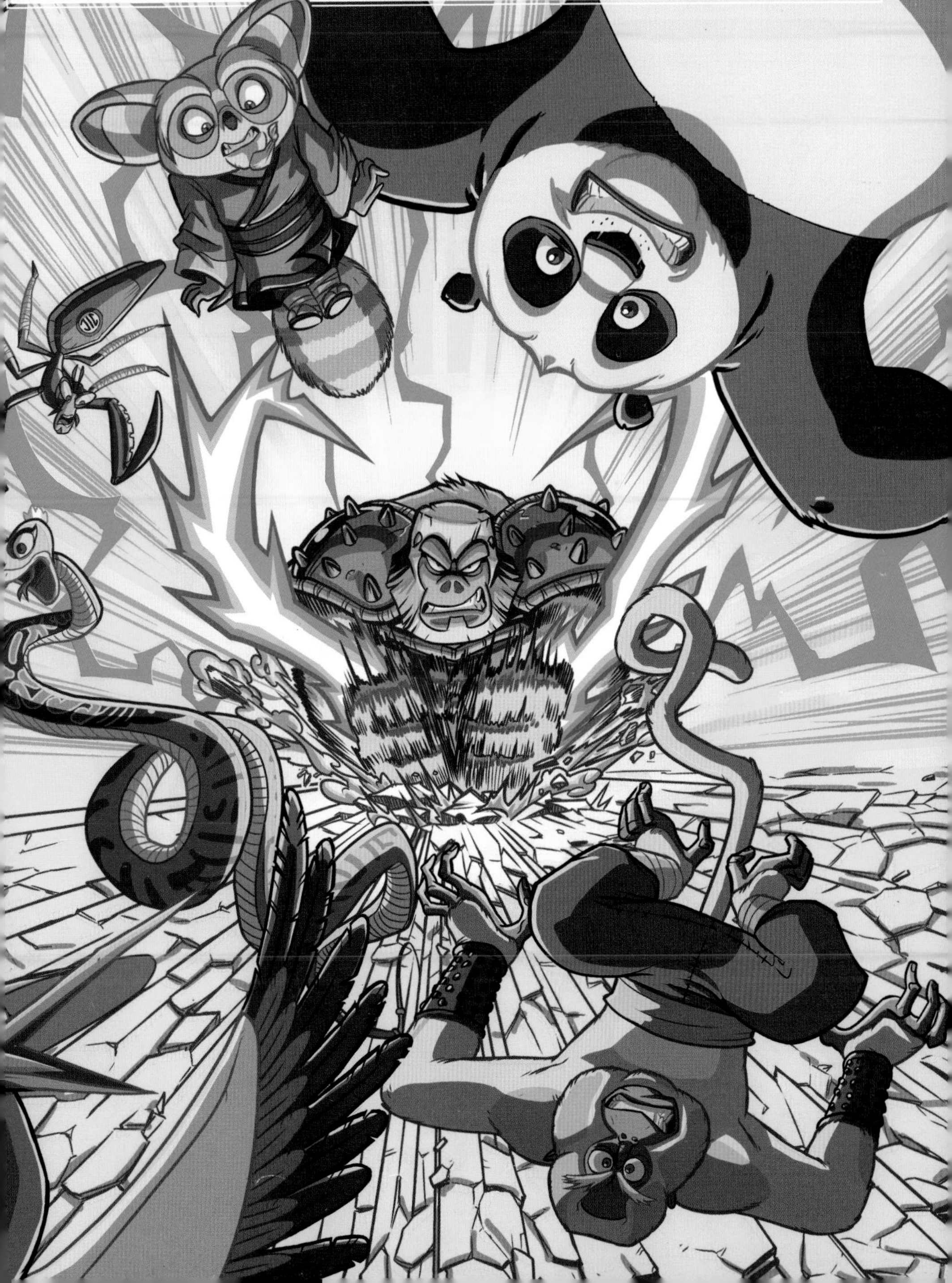

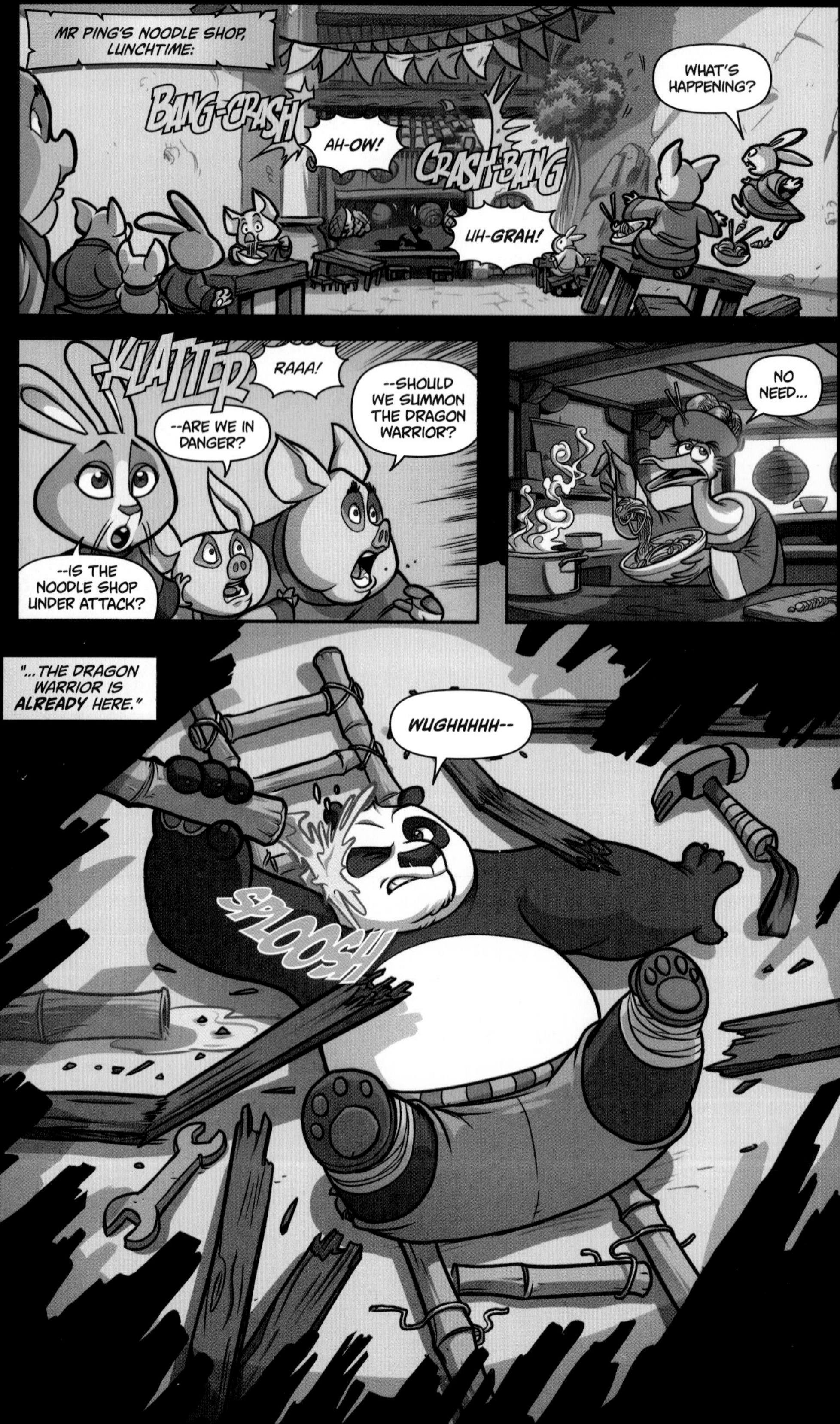
MR PING'S NOODLE SHOP, LUNCHTIME:
BANG-CRASH!
AH-OW!
CRASH-BANG
UH-GRAH!
WHAT'S HAPPENING?
-KLATTER
RAAA!
--ARE WE IN DANGER?
--SHOULD WE SUMMON THE DRAGON WARRIOR?
--IS THE NOODLE SHOP UNDER ATTACK?
NO NEED...
"...THE DRAGON WARRIOR IS ALREADY HERE."
WUGHHHHH--
SPLOOSH

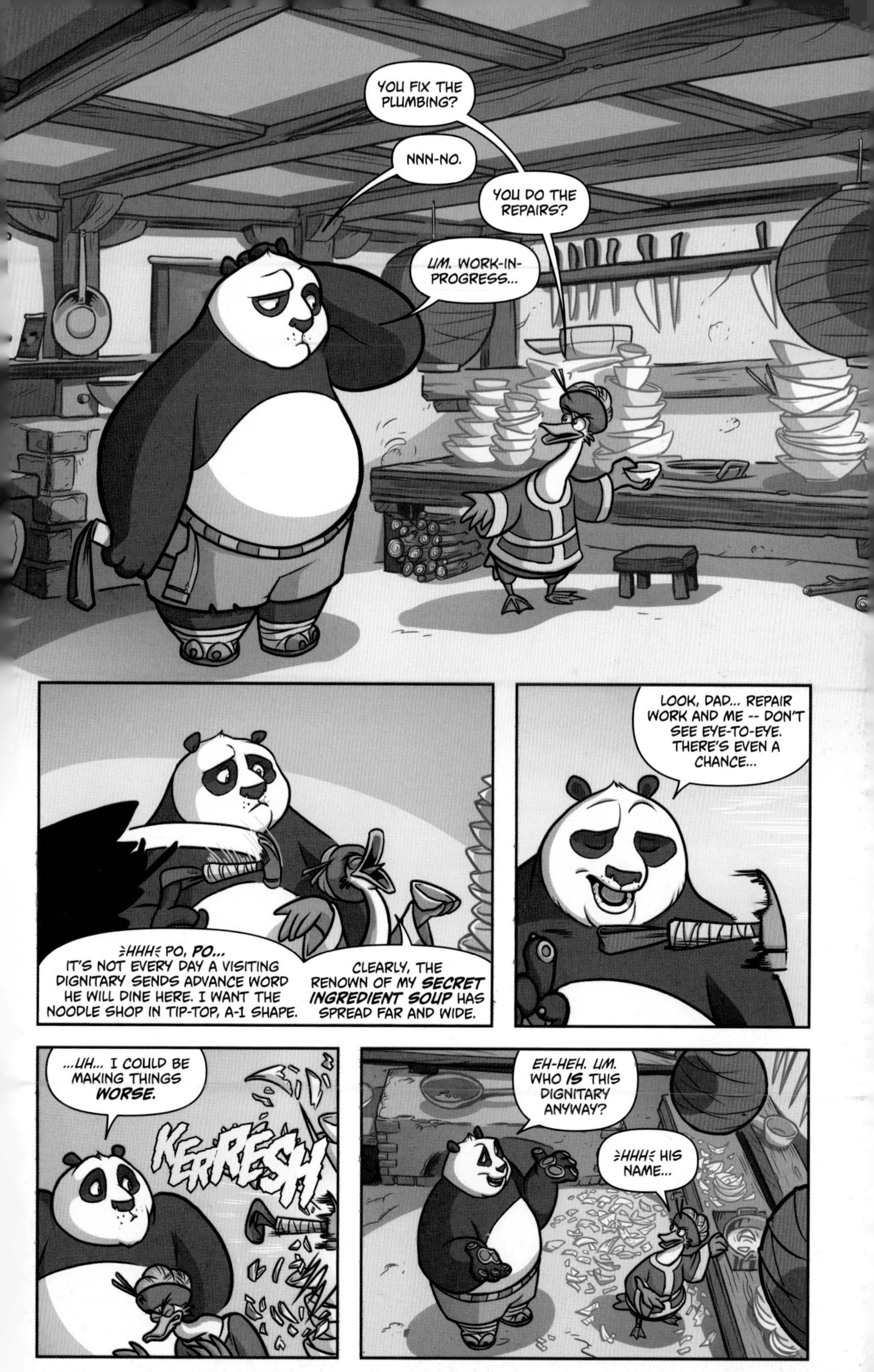
YOU FIX THE PLUMBING?
NNN-NO.
YOU DO THE REPAIRS?
UM. WORK-IN-PROGRESS...
⪢HHH⪡ PO, PO... IT'S NOT EVERY DAY A VISITING DIGNITARY SENDS ADVANCE WORD HE WILL DINE HERE. I WANT THE NOODLE SHOP IN TIP-TOP, A-1 SHAPE.
CLEARLY, THE RENOWN OF MY SECRET INGREDIENT SOUP HAS SPREAD FAR AND WIDE.
LOOK, DAD... REPAIR WORK AND ME -- DON'T SEE EYE-TO-EYE. THERE'S EVEN A CHANCE...
...UH... I COULD BE MAKING THINGS WORSE.
KERRESH
EH-HEH. UM. WHO IS THIS DIGNITARY ANYWAY?
⪢HHH⪡ HIS NAME...

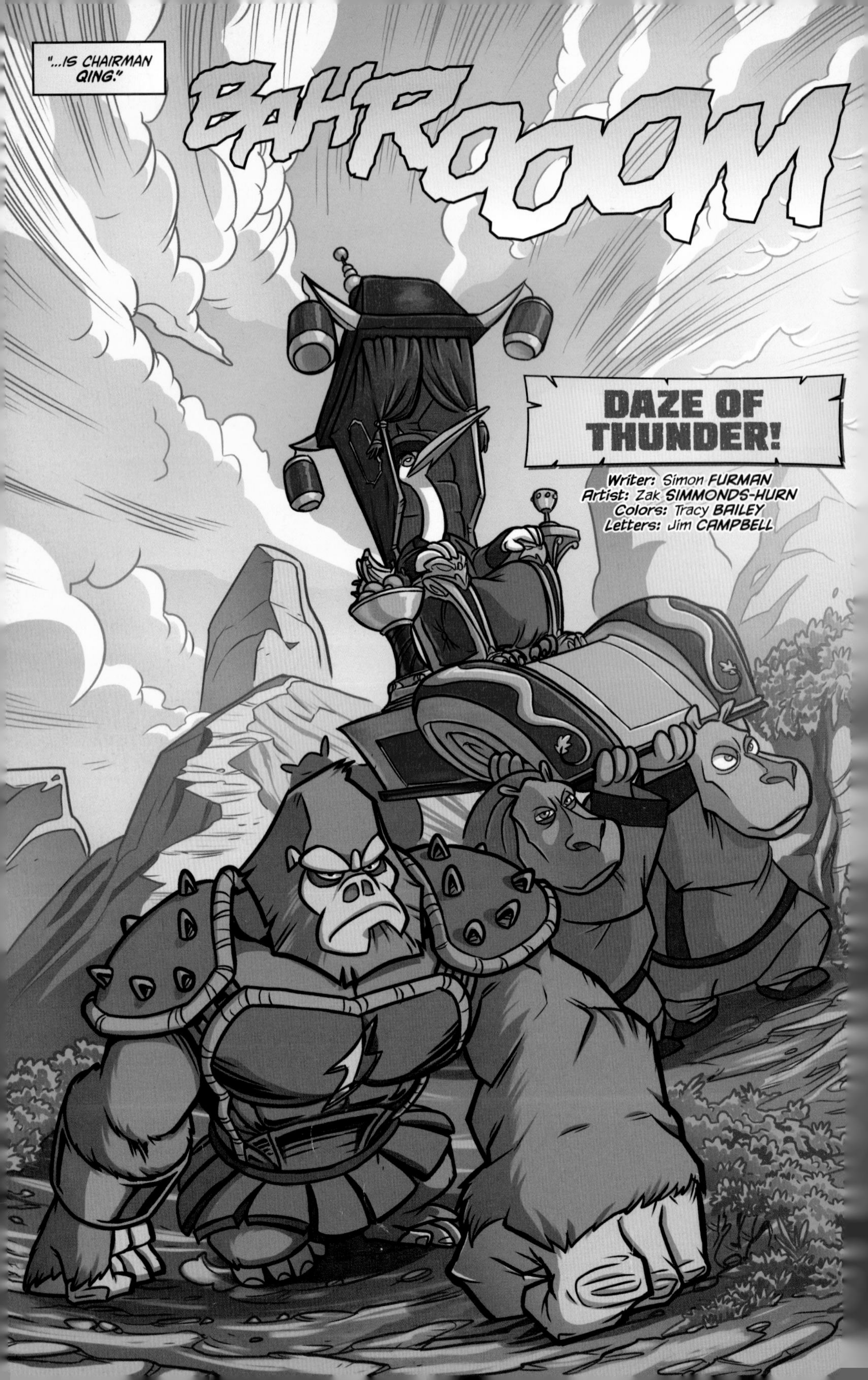
"...IS CHAIRMAN QING."
BAHROOOM
DAZE OF THUNDER!
Writer: Simon FURMAN
Artist: Zak SIMMONDS-HURN
Colors: Tracy BAILEY
Letters: Jim CAMPBELL

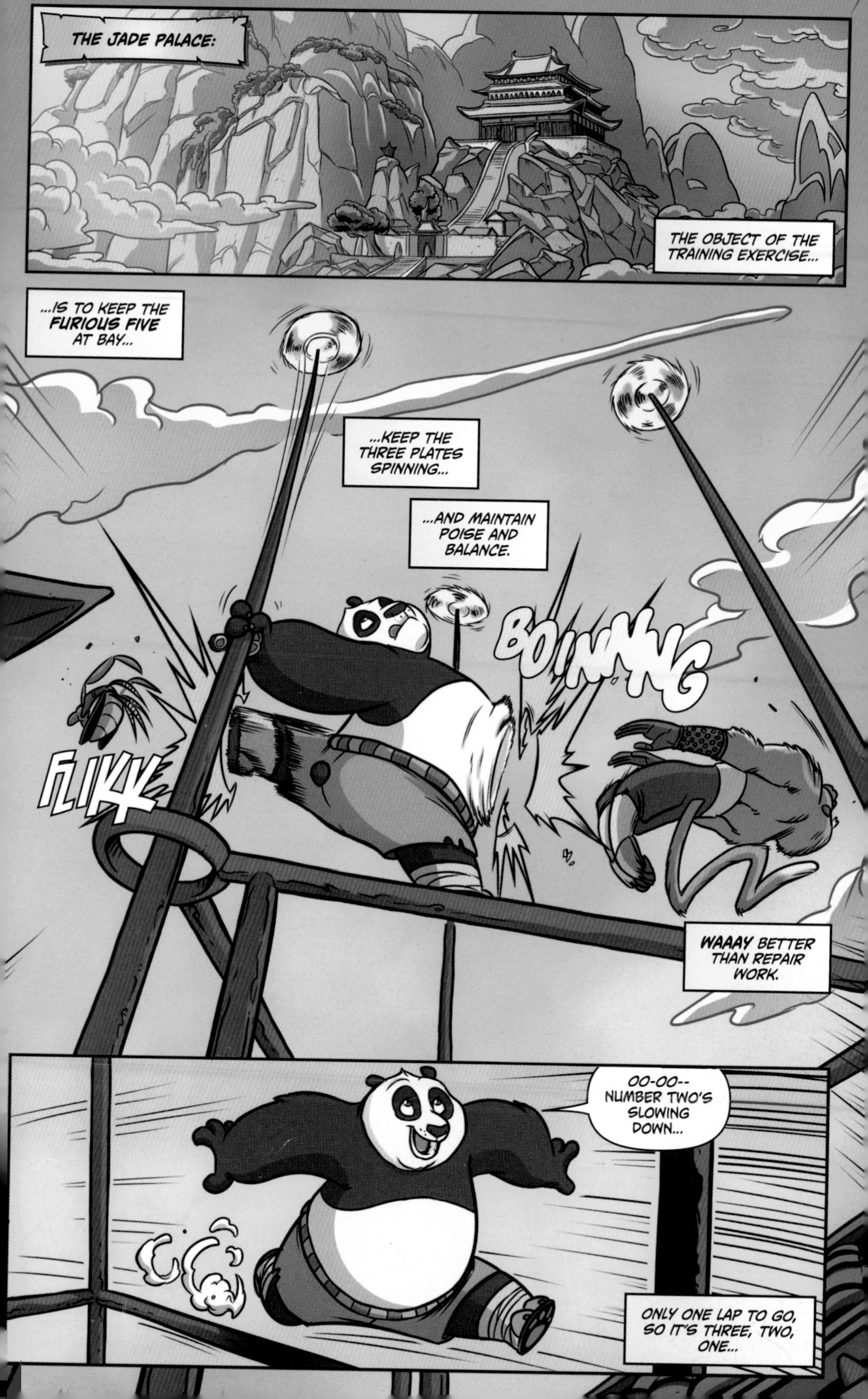
THE JADE PALACE:
THE OBJECT OF THE TRAINING EXERCISE...
...IS TO KEEP THE **FURIOUS FIVE** AT BAY...
...KEEP THE THREE PLATES SPINNING...
...AND MAINTAIN POISE AND BALANCE.
BOINNNG
FLIKK
WAAAY BETTER THAN REPAIR WORK.
OO-OO-- NUMBER TWO'S SLOWING DOWN...
ONLY ONE LAP TO GO, SO IT'S THREE, TWO, ONE...

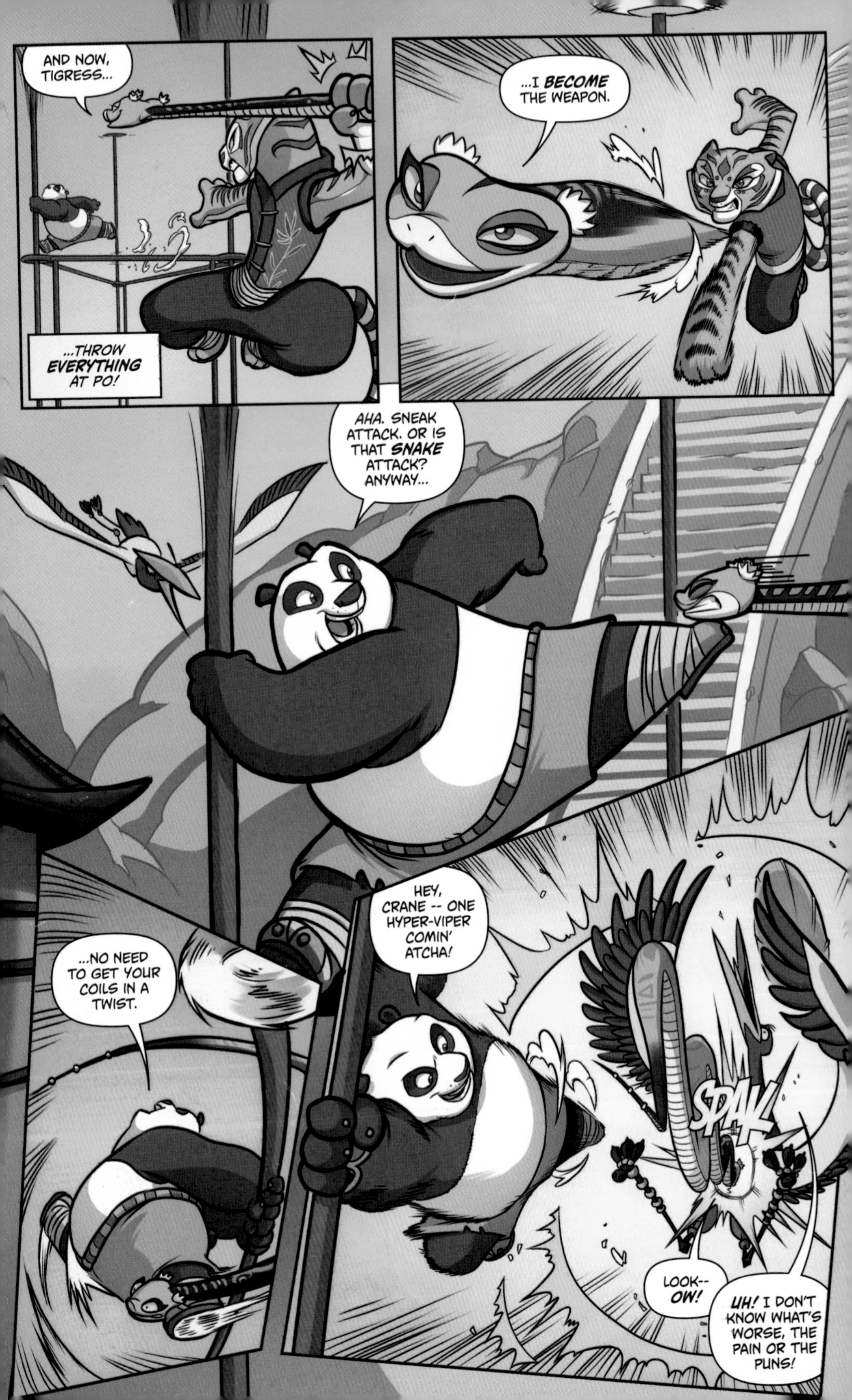
AND NOW, TIGRESS...
...THROW EVERYTHING AT PO!
...I BECOME THE WEAPON.
AHA. SNEAK ATTACK. OR IS THAT SNAKE ATTACK? ANYWAY...
...NO NEED TO GET YOUR COILS IN A TWIST.
HEY, CRANE -- ONE HYPER-VIPER COMIN' ATCHA!
SPAK!
LOOK-- OW!
UH! I DON'T KNOW WHAT'S WORSE, THE PAIN OR THE PUNS!

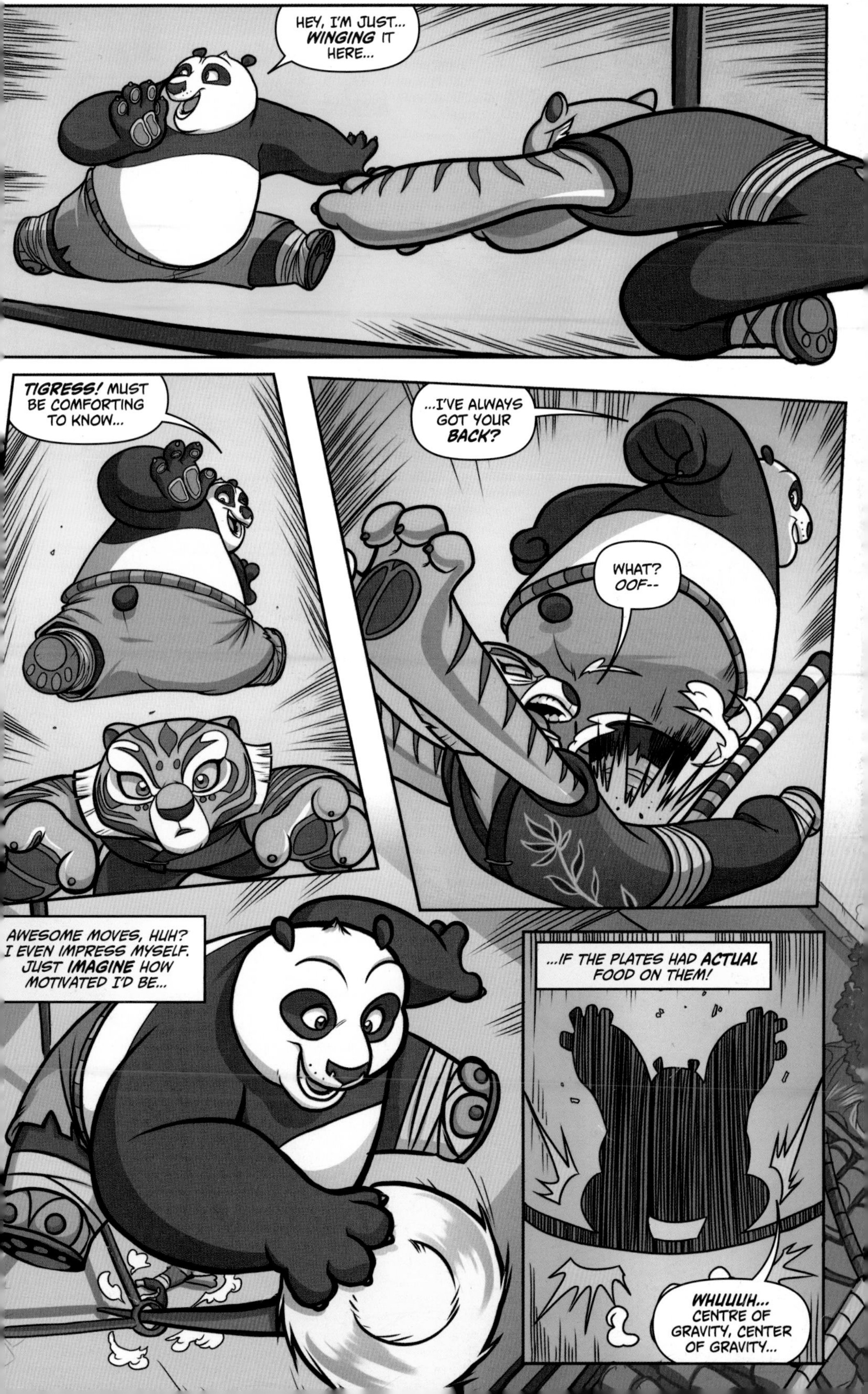
HEY, I'M JUST... WINGING IT HERE...
TIGRESS! MUST BE COMFORTING TO KNOW...
...I'VE ALWAYS GOT YOUR BACK?
WHAT? OOF--
AWESOME MOVES, HUH? I EVEN IMPRESS MYSELF. JUST IMAGINE HOW MOTIVATED I'D BE...
...IF THE PLATES HAD ACTUAL FOOD ON THEM!
WHUUUH... CENTRE OF GRAVITY, CENTER OF GRAVITY...

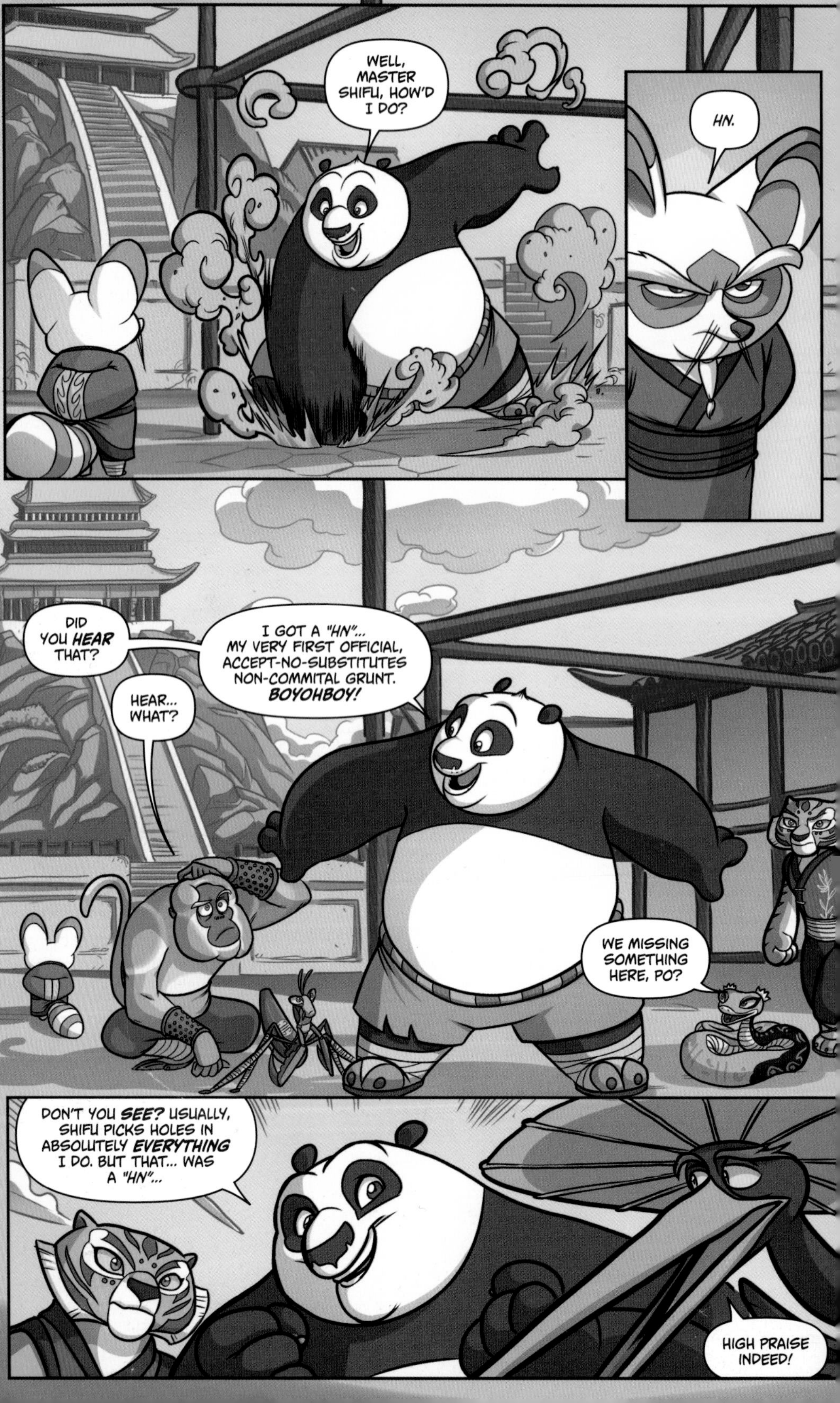
WELL, MASTER SHIFU, HOW'D I DO?
HN.
DID YOU **HEAR** THAT?
I GOT A "HN"... MY VERY FIRST OFFICIAL, ACCEPT-NO-SUBSTITUTES NON-COMMITAL GRUNT. ***BOYOHBOY!***
HEAR... WHAT?
WE MISSING SOMETHING HERE, PO?
DON'T YOU ***SEE?*** USUALLY, SHIFU PICKS HOLES IN ABSOLUTELY ***EVERYTHING*** I DO. BUT THAT... WAS A "HN"...
HIGH PRAISE INDEED!

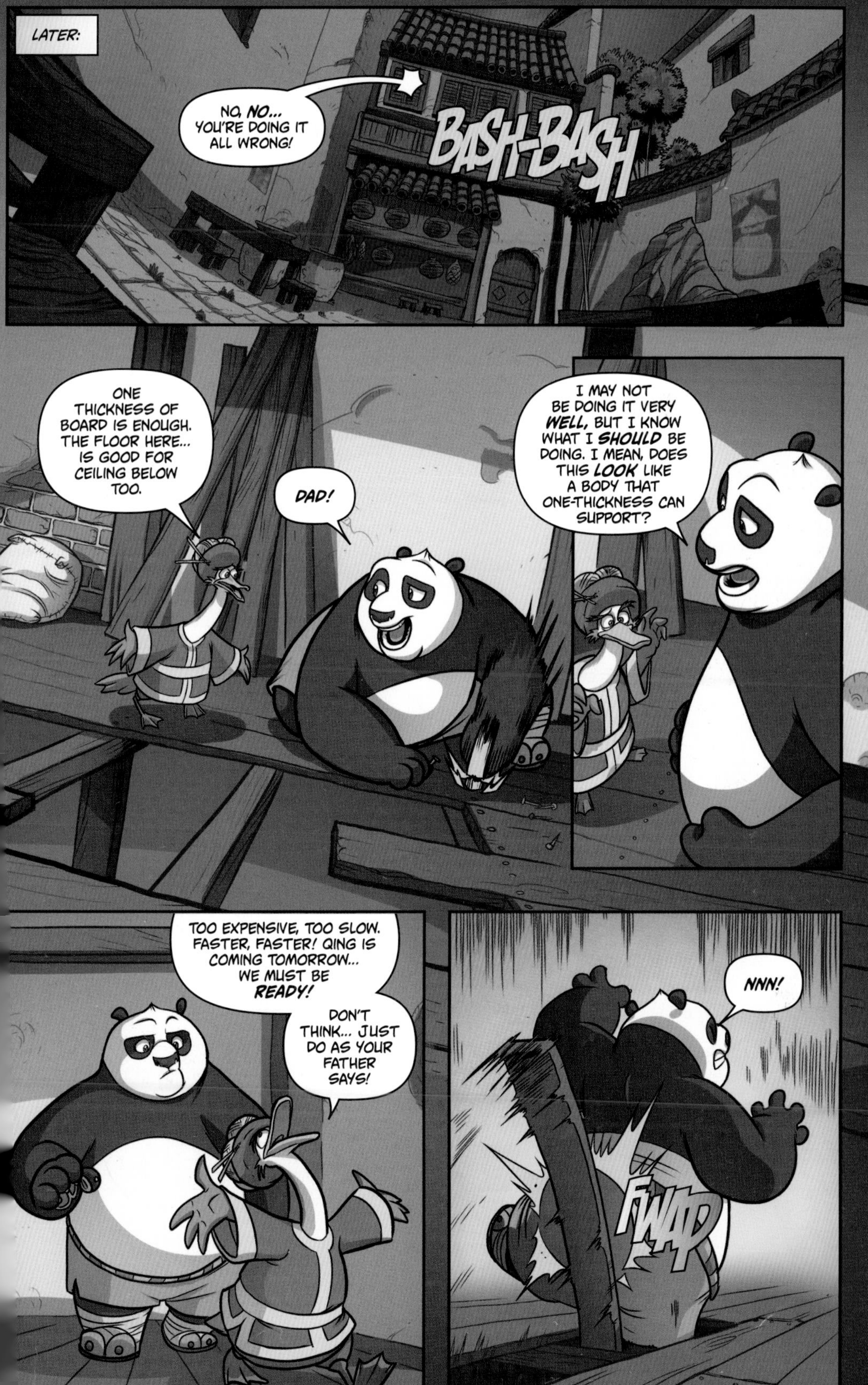
LATER:
NO, NO... YOU'RE DOING IT ALL WRONG!
BASH-BASH
ONE THICKNESS OF BOARD IS ENOUGH. THE FLOOR HERE... IS GOOD FOR CEILING BELOW TOO.
DAD!
I MAY NOT BE DOING IT VERY WELL, BUT I KNOW WHAT I SHOULD BE DOING. I MEAN, DOES THIS LOOK LIKE A BODY THAT ONE-THICKNESS CAN SUPPORT?
TOO EXPENSIVE, TOO SLOW. FASTER, FASTER! QING IS COMING TOMORROW... WE MUST BE READY!
DON'T THINK... JUST DO AS YOUR FATHER SAYS!
NNN!
FWAP

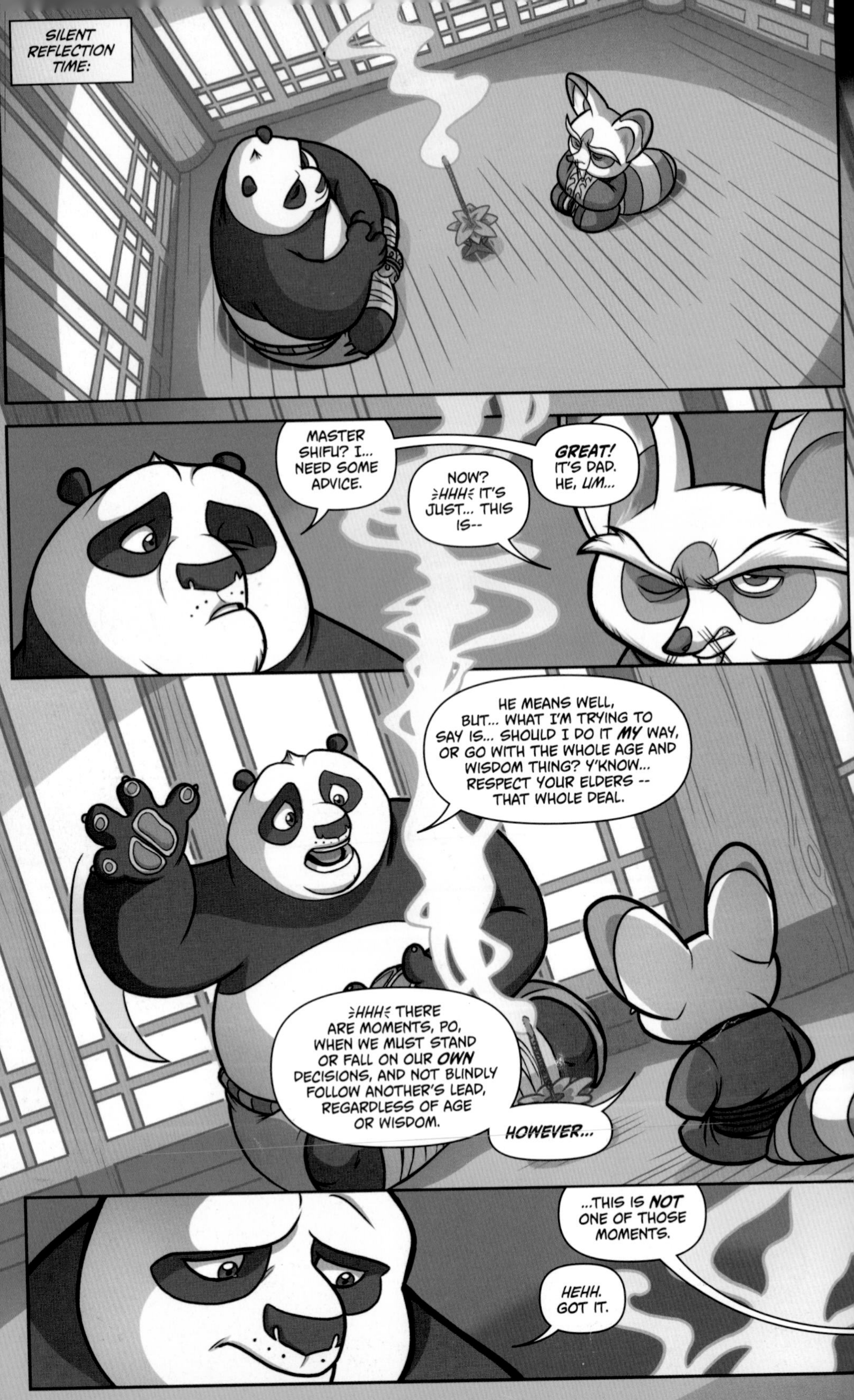

SILENT REFLECTION TIME:
MASTER SHIFU? I... NEED SOME ADVICE.
NOW? ≡HHH≡ IT'S JUST... THIS IS--
GREAT! IT'S DAD. HE, UM...
HE MEANS WELL, BUT... WHAT I'M TRYING TO SAY IS... SHOULD I DO IT MY WAY, OR GO WITH THE WHOLE AGE AND WISDOM THING? Y'KNOW... RESPECT YOUR ELDERS -- THAT WHOLE DEAL.
≡HHH≡ THERE ARE MOMENTS, PO, WHEN WE MUST STAND OR FALL ON OUR OWN DECISIONS, AND NOT BLINDLY FOLLOW ANOTHER'S LEAD, REGARDLESS OF AGE OR WISDOM.
HOWEVER...
...THIS IS NOT ONE OF THOSE MOMENTS.
HEHH. GOT IT.

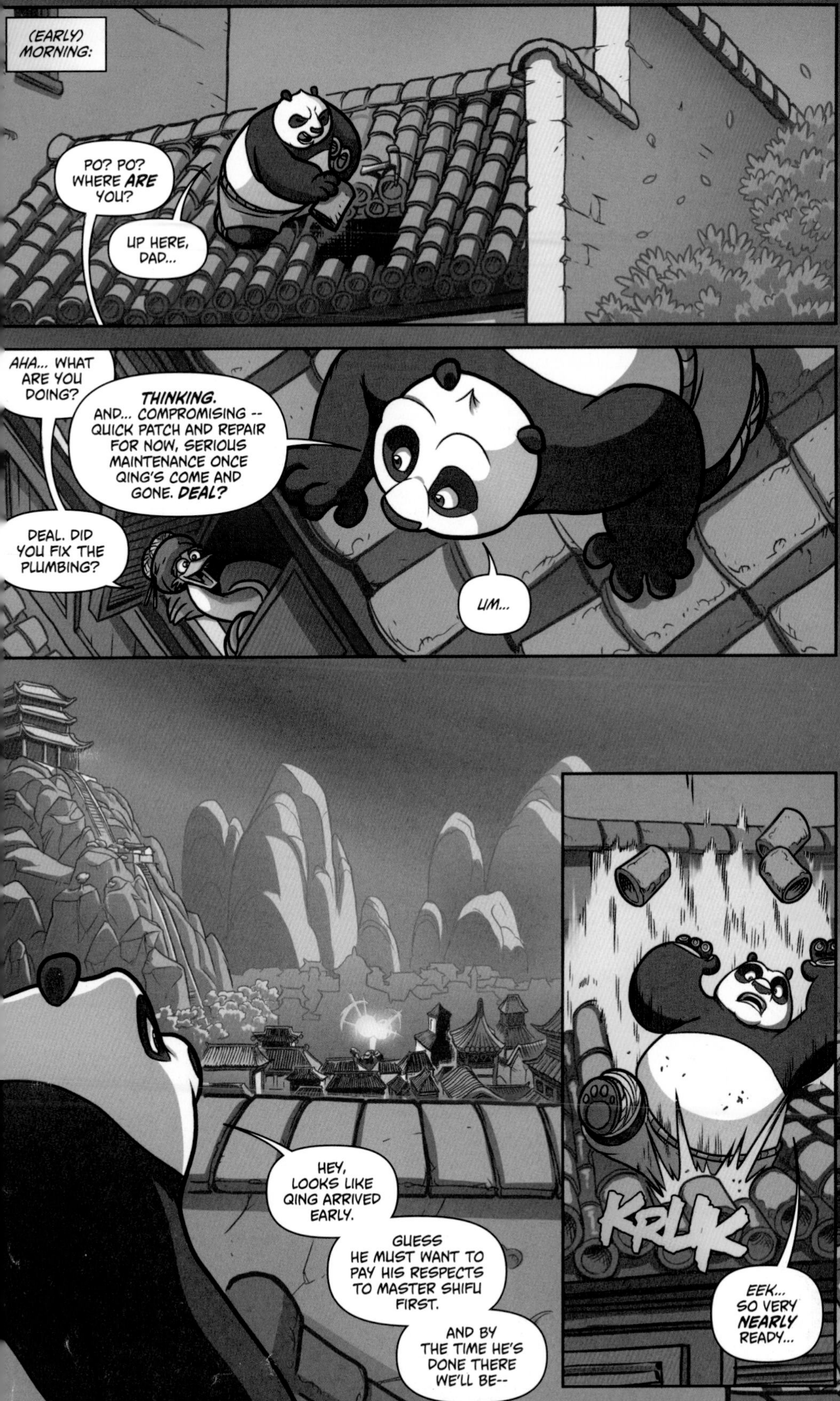

(EARLY) MORNING:
PO? PO? WHERE ARE YOU?
UP HERE, DAD...
AHA... WHAT ARE YOU DOING?
THINKING. AND... COMPROMISING -- QUICK PATCH AND REPAIR FOR NOW, SERIOUS MAINTENANCE ONCE QING'S COME AND GONE. DEAL?
DEAL. DID YOU FIX THE PLUMBING?
UM...
HEY, LOOKS LIKE QING ARRIVED EARLY.
GUESS HE MUST WANT TO PAY HIS RESPECTS TO MASTER SHIFU FIRST.
AND BY THE TIME HE'S DONE THERE WE'LL BE--
KRUK
EEK... SO VERY NEARLY READY...

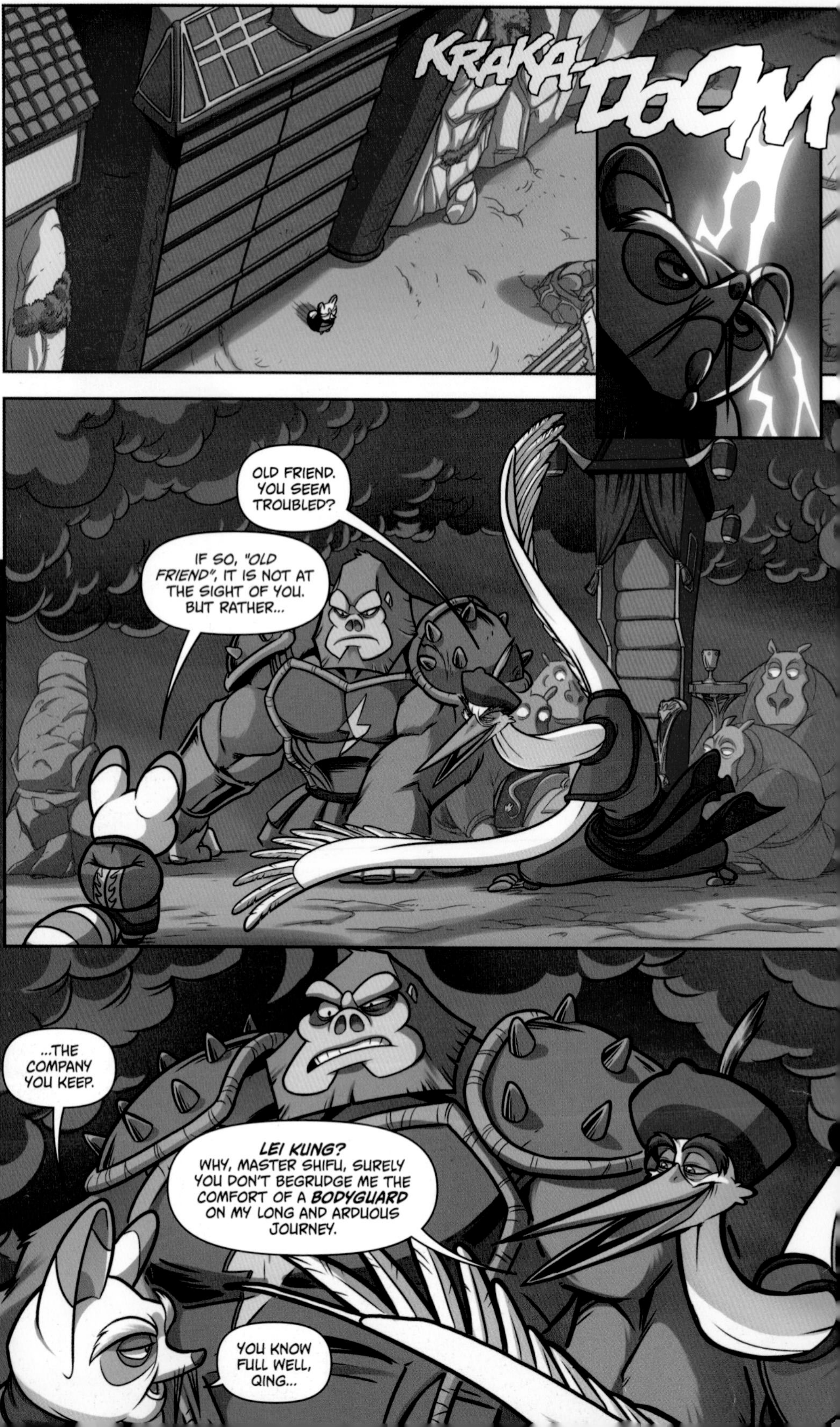
KRAKA-DOOM
OLD FRIEND. YOU SEEM TROUBLED?
IF SO, "OLD FRIEND", IT IS NOT AT THE SIGHT OF YOU. BUT RATHER...
...THE COMPANY YOU KEEP.
LEI KUNG? WHY, MASTER SHIFU, SURELY YOU DON'T BEGRUDGE ME THE COMFORT OF A BODYGUARD ON MY LONG AND ARDUOUS JOURNEY.
YOU KNOW FULL WELL, QING...

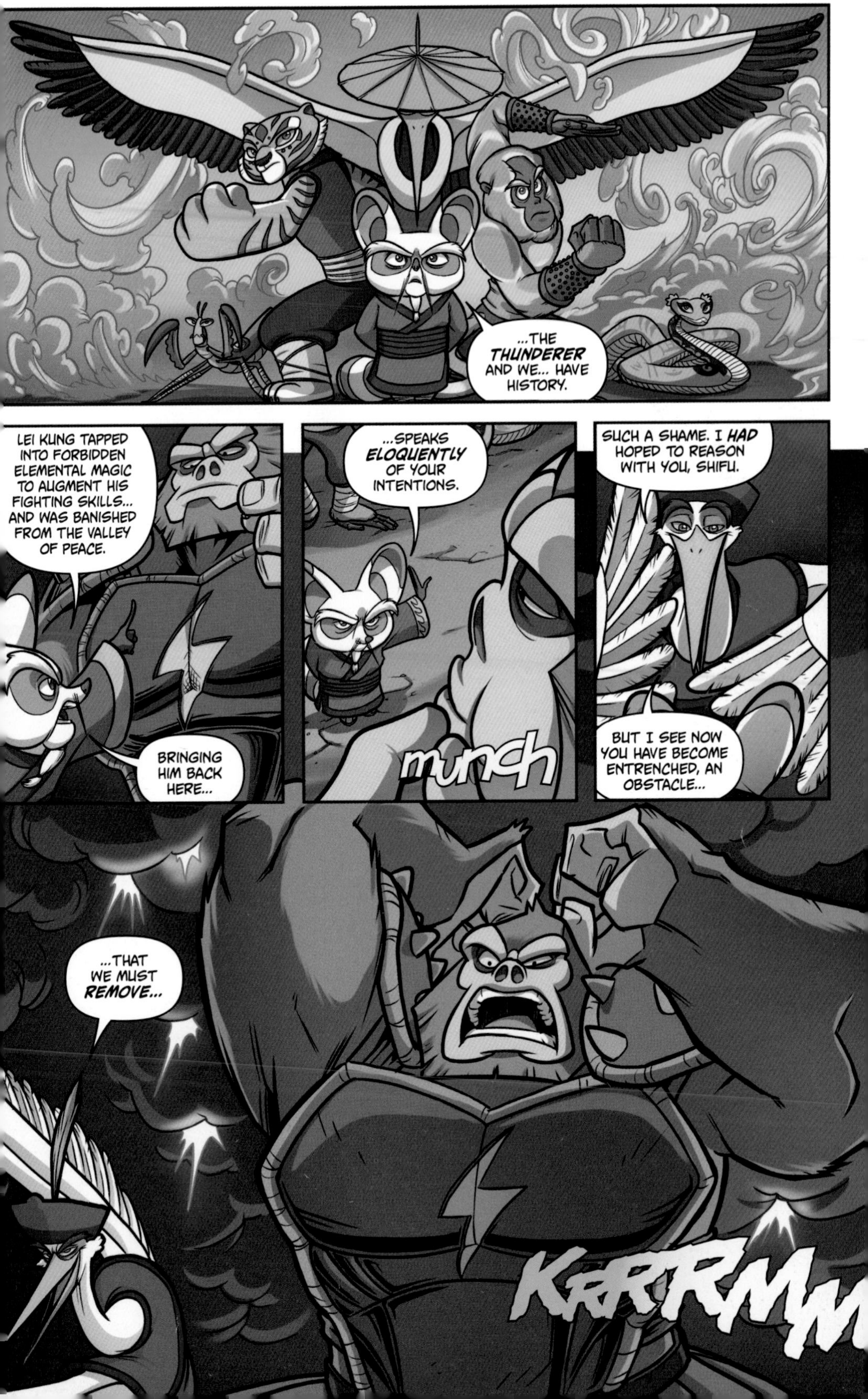
...THE THUNDERER AND WE... HAVE HISTORY.
LEI KUNG TAPPED INTO FORBIDDEN ELEMENTAL MAGIC TO AUGMENT HIS FIGHTING SKILLS... AND WAS BANISHED FROM THE VALLEY OF PEACE.
BRINGING HIM BACK HERE...
...SPEAKS ELOQUENTLY OF YOUR INTENTIONS.
munch
SUCH A SHAME. I HAD HOPED TO REASON WITH YOU, SHIFU.
BUT I SEE NOW YOU HAVE BECOME ENTRENCHED, AN OBSTACLE...
...THAT WE MUST REMOVE...
KRRRMM

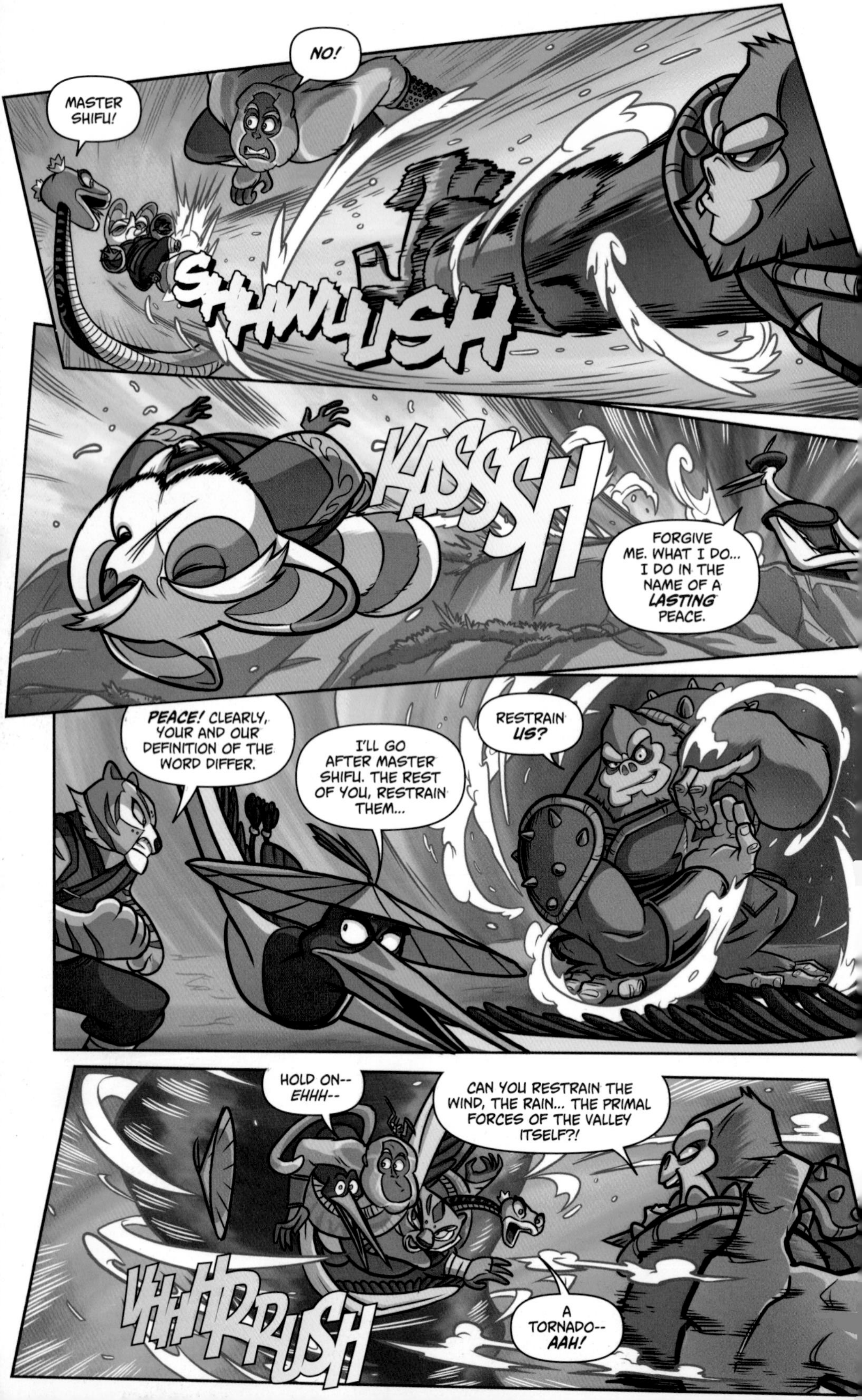
MASTER SHIFU!
NO!
SHHWUSH
KASSSH
FORGIVE ME. WHAT I DO... I DO IN THE NAME OF A *LASTING* PEACE.
PEACE! CLEARLY, YOUR AND OUR DEFINITION OF THE WORD DIFFER.
I'LL GO AFTER MASTER SHIFU. THE REST OF YOU, RESTRAIN THEM...
RESTRAIN *US?*
HOLD ON-- EHHH--
CAN YOU RESTRAIN THE WIND, THE RAIN... THE PRIMAL FORCES OF THE VALLEY ITSELF?!
VHHRRUSH
A TORNADO-- *AAH!*

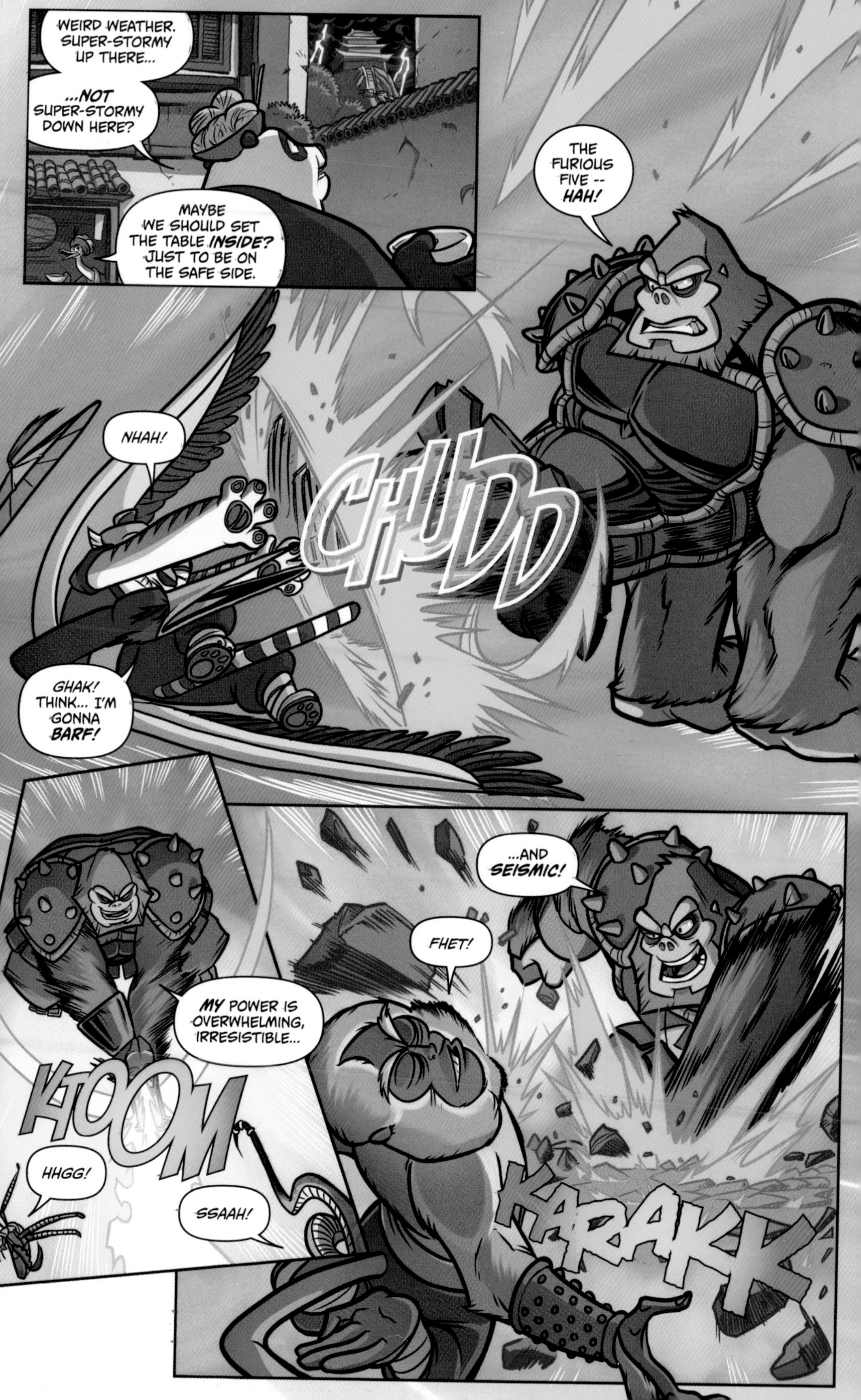
WEIRD WEATHER. SUPER-STORMY UP THERE...
...NOT SUPER-STORMY DOWN HERE?
MAYBE WE SHOULD SET THE TABLE INSIDE? JUST TO BE ON THE SAFE SIDE.
THE FURIOUS FIVE -- HAH!
NHAH!
CHUDD
GHAK! THINK... I'M GONNA BARF!
MY POWER IS OVERWHELMING, IRRESISTIBLE...
KTOOM
HHGG!
SSAAH!
...AND SEISMIC!
FHET!
KARAKK

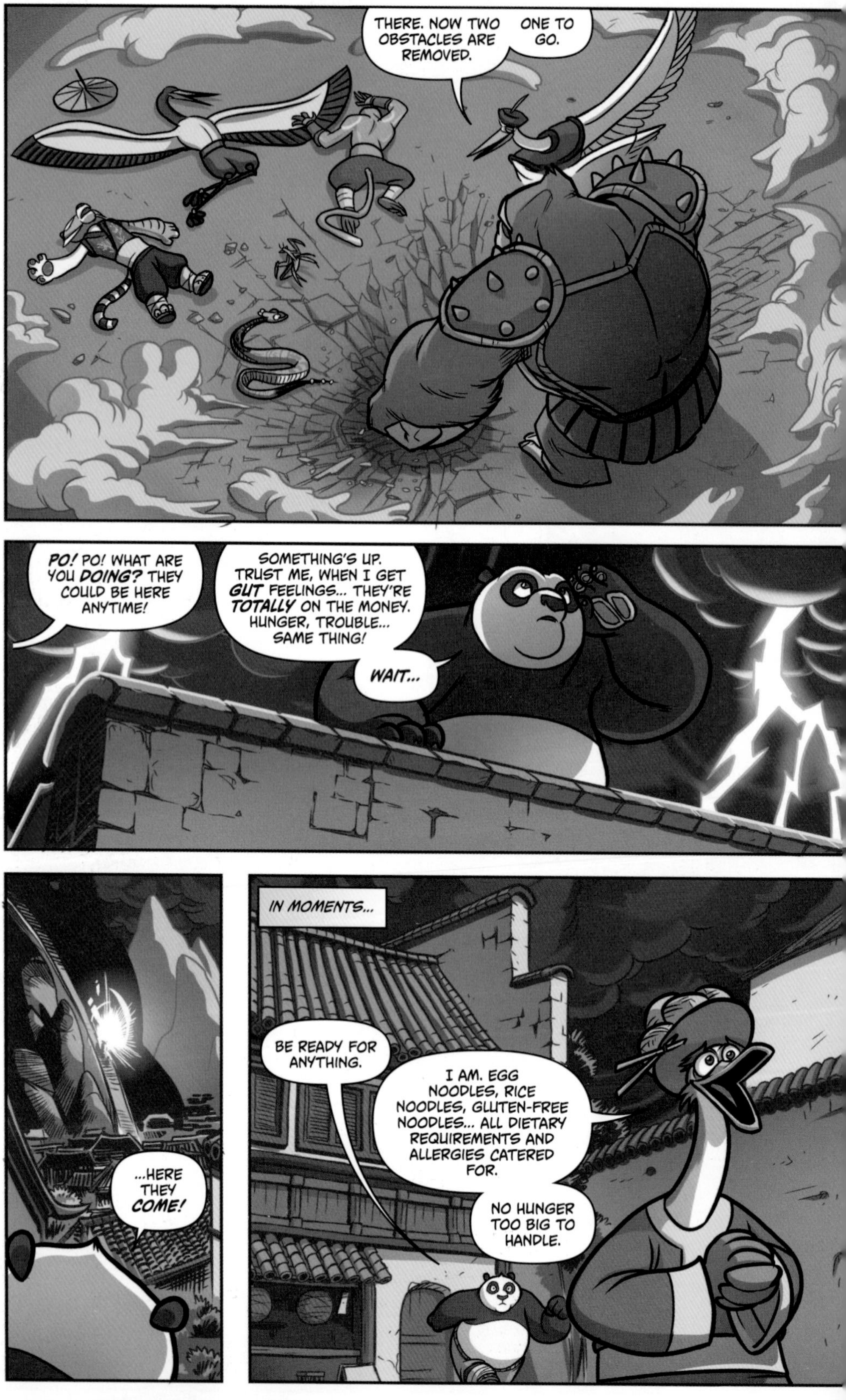
THERE. NOW TWO OBSTACLES ARE REMOVED.
ONE TO GO.
PO! PO! WHAT ARE YOU DOING? THEY COULD BE HERE ANYTIME!
SOMETHING'S UP. TRUST ME, WHEN I GET GUT FEELINGS... THEY'RE TOTALLY ON THE MONEY. HUNGER, TROUBLE... SAME THING!
WAIT...
...HERE THEY COME!
IN MOMENTS...
BE READY FOR ANYTHING.
I AM. EGG NOODLES, RICE NOODLES, GLUTEN-FREE NOODLES... ALL DIETARY REQUIREMENTS AND ALLERGIES CATERED FOR.
NO HUNGER TOO BIG TO HANDLE.

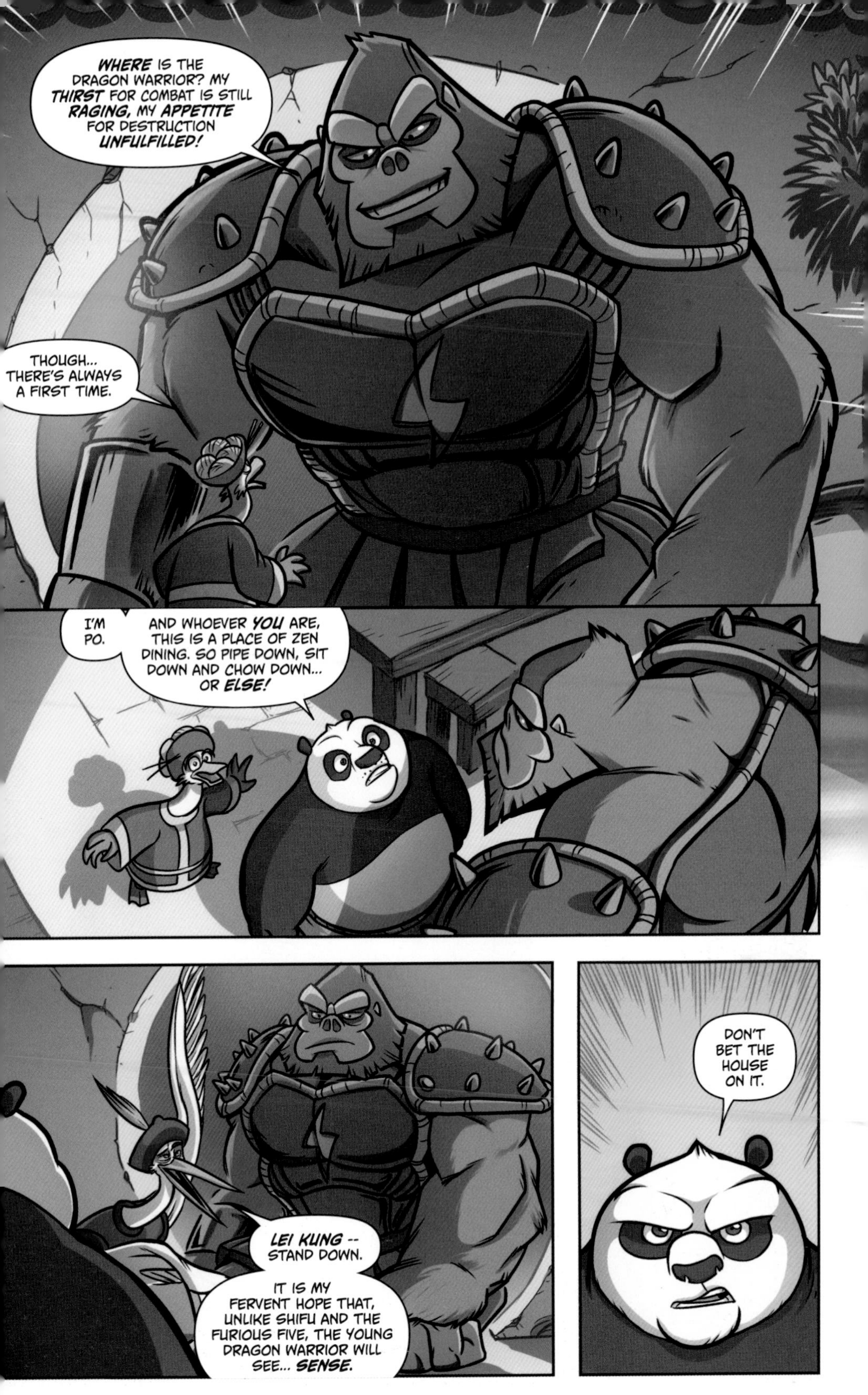
WHERE IS THE DRAGON WARRIOR? MY THIRST FOR COMBAT IS STILL RAGING, MY APPETITE FOR DESTRUCTION UNFULFILLED!
THOUGH... THERE'S ALWAYS A FIRST TIME.
I'M PO.
AND WHOEVER YOU ARE, THIS IS A PLACE OF ZEN DINING. SO PIPE DOWN, SIT DOWN AND CHOW DOWN... OR ELSE!
LEI KUNG -- STAND DOWN.
IT IS MY FERVENT HOPE THAT, UNLIKE SHIFU AND THE FURIOUS FIVE, THE YOUNG DRAGON WARRIOR WILL SEE... SENSE.
DON'T BET THE HOUSE ON IT.

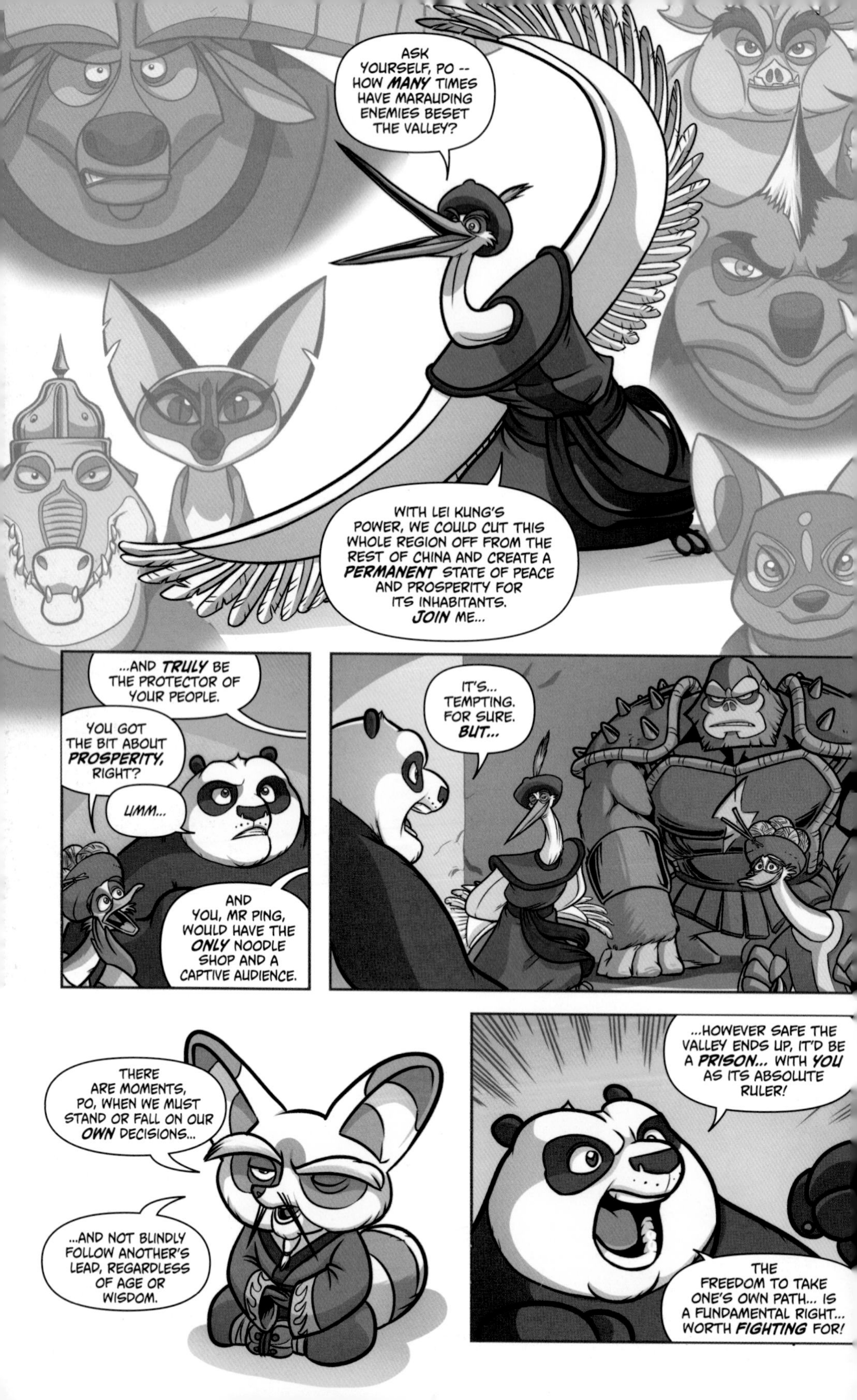
ASK YOURSELF, PO -- HOW MANY TIMES HAVE MARAUDING ENEMIES BESET THE VALLEY?
WITH LEI KUNG'S POWER, WE COULD CUT THIS WHOLE REGION OFF FROM THE REST OF CHINA AND CREATE A PERMANENT STATE OF PEACE AND PROSPERITY FOR ITS INHABITANTS. JOIN ME...
...AND TRULY BE THE PROTECTOR OF YOUR PEOPLE.
YOU GOT THE BIT ABOUT PROSPERITY, RIGHT?
UMM...
AND YOU, MR PING, WOULD HAVE THE ONLY NOODLE SHOP AND A CAPTIVE AUDIENCE.
IT'S... TEMPTING. FOR SURE. BUT...
THERE ARE MOMENTS, PO, WHEN WE MUST STAND OR FALL ON OUR OWN DECISIONS...
...AND NOT BLINDLY FOLLOW ANOTHER'S LEAD, REGARDLESS OF AGE OR WISDOM.
...HOWEVER SAFE THE VALLEY ENDS UP, IT'D BE A PRISON... WITH YOU AS ITS ABSOLUTE RULER!
THE FREEDOM TO TAKE ONE'S OWN PATH... IS A FUNDAMENTAL RIGHT... WORTH FIGHTING FOR!

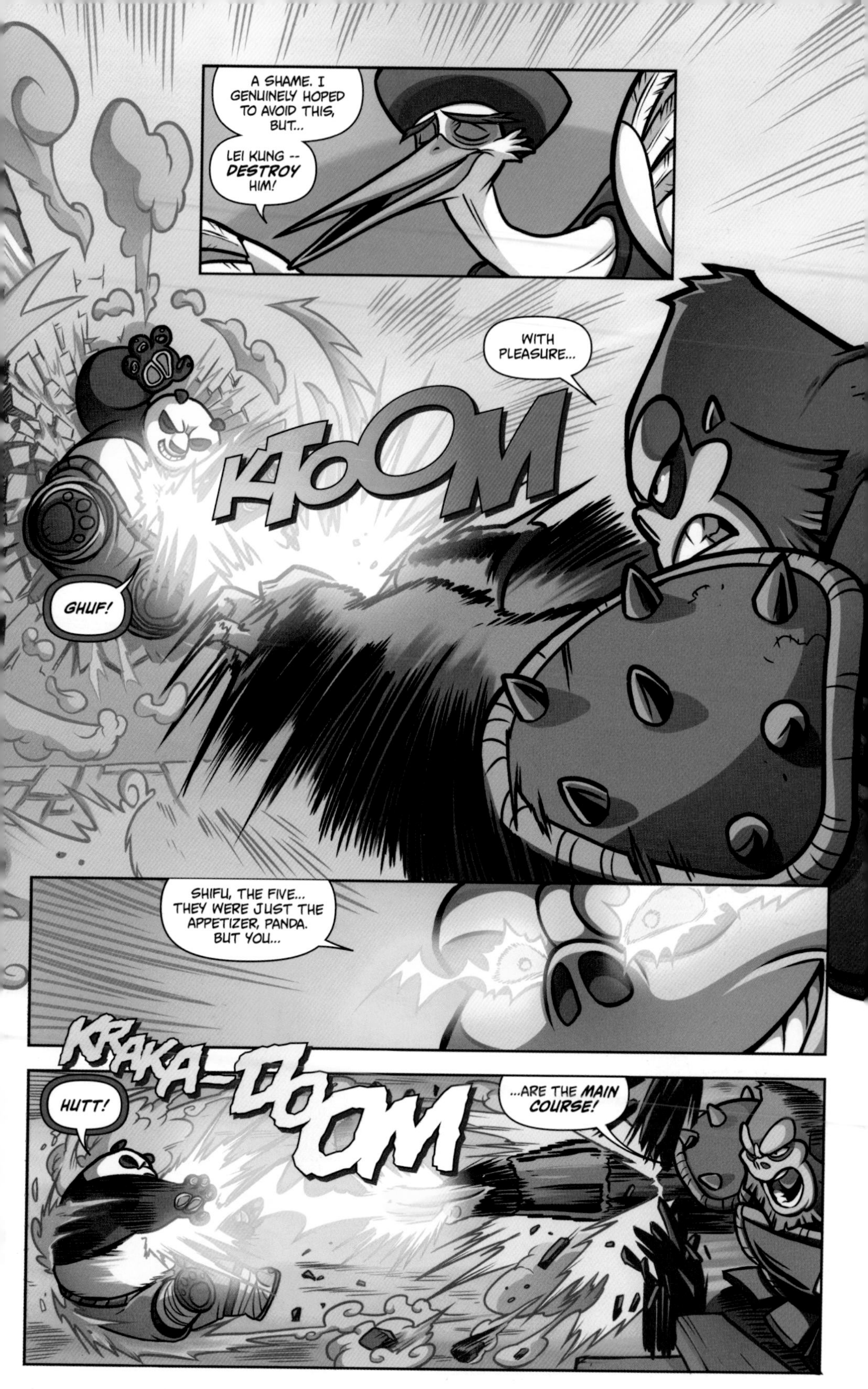
A SHAME. I GENUINELY HOPED TO AVOID THIS, BUT...
LEI KUNG -- DESTROY HIM!
WITH PLEASURE...
KTOOM
GHUF!
SHIFU, THE FIVE... THEY WERE JUST THE APPETIZER, PANDA. BUT YOU...
KRAKA-DOOM
HUTT!
...ARE THE MAIN COURSE!

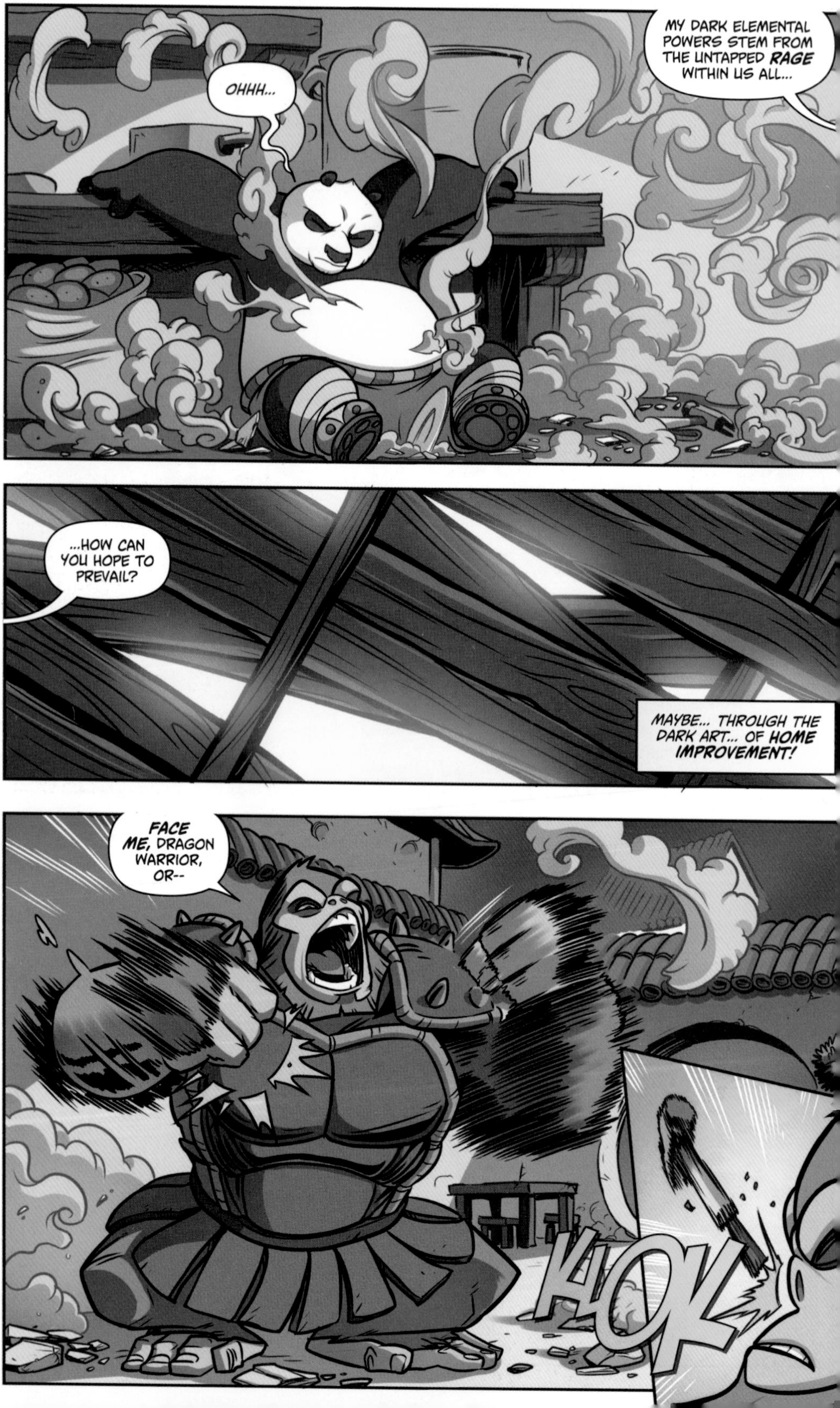
OHHH...
MY DARK ELEMENTAL POWERS STEM FROM THE UNTAPPED RAGE WITHIN US ALL...
...HOW CAN YOU HOPE TO PREVAIL?
MAYBE... THROUGH THE DARK ART... OF HOME IMPROVEMENT!
FACE ME, DRAGON WARRIOR, OR--
KLOK

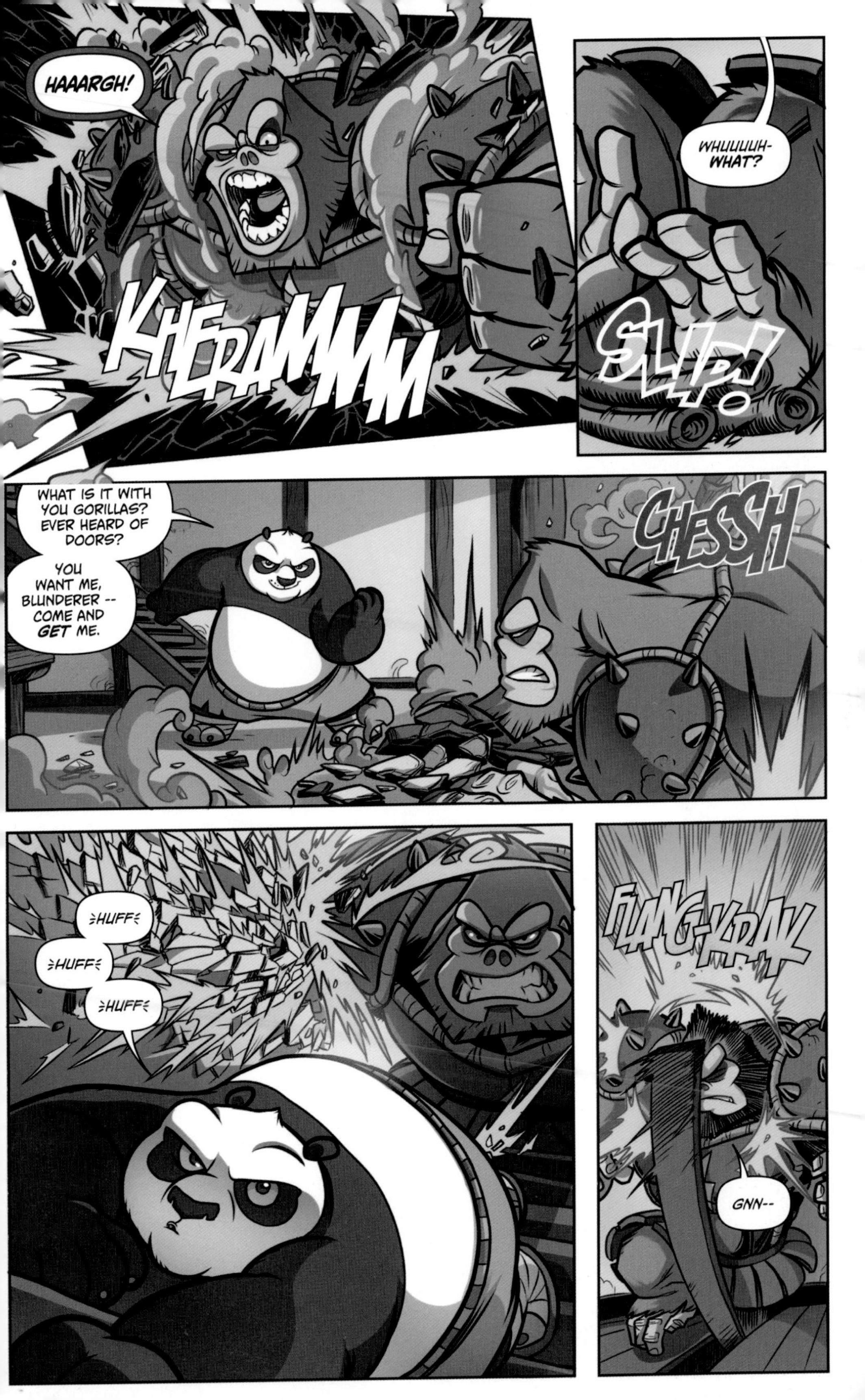
HAAARGH!
KHERAMMMM
WHUUUUH-WHAT?
SLIP!
WHAT IS IT WITH YOU GORILLAS? EVER HEARD OF DOORS?
YOU WANT ME, BLUNDERER -- COME AND GET ME.
CHESSH
HUFF
HUFF
HUFF
FLANG-KRAK
GNN--

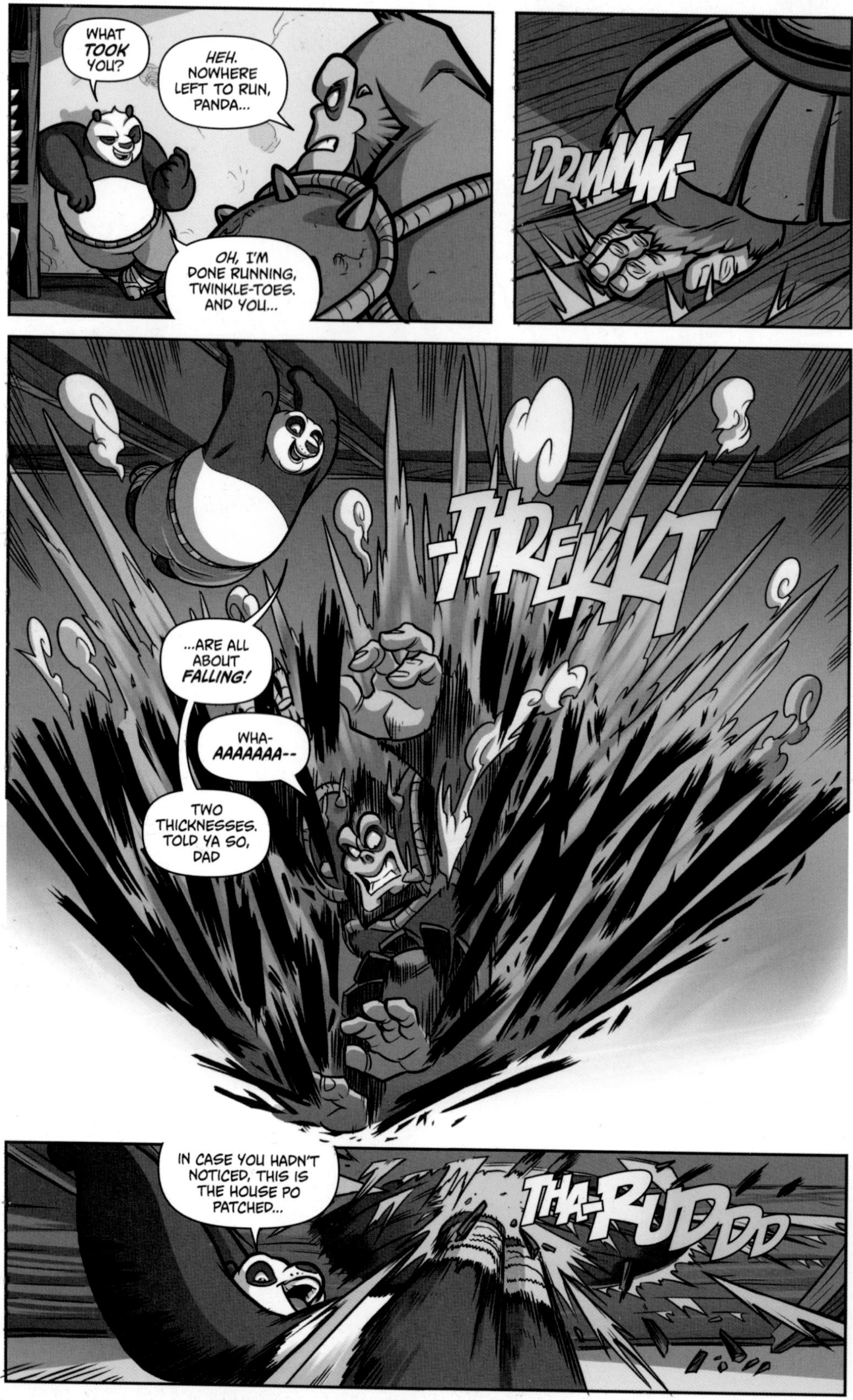

WHAT TOOK YOU?
HEH. NOWHERE LEFT TO RUN, PANDA...
OH, I'M DONE RUNNING, TWINKLE-TOES. AND YOU...
DRMMM-
-THREKKT
...ARE ALL ABOUT FALLING!
WHA-AAAAAAA--
TWO THICKNESSES. TOLD YA SO, DAD
IN CASE YOU HADN'T NOTICED, THIS IS THE HOUSE PO PATCHED...
THA-RUDDD

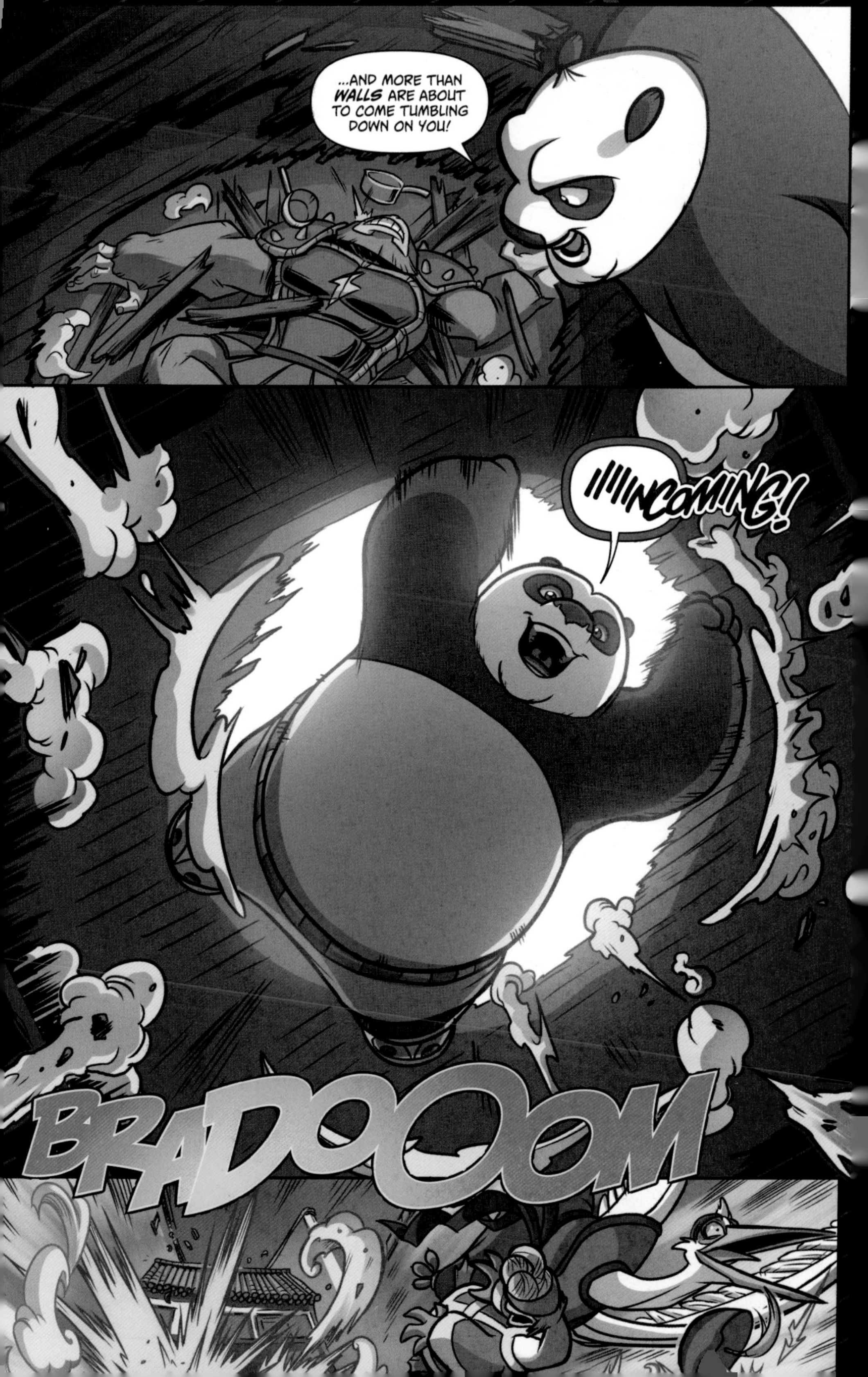
...AND MORE THAN WALLS ARE ABOUT TO COME TUMBLING DOWN ON YOU!
I'''NCOMING!
BRADOOOM

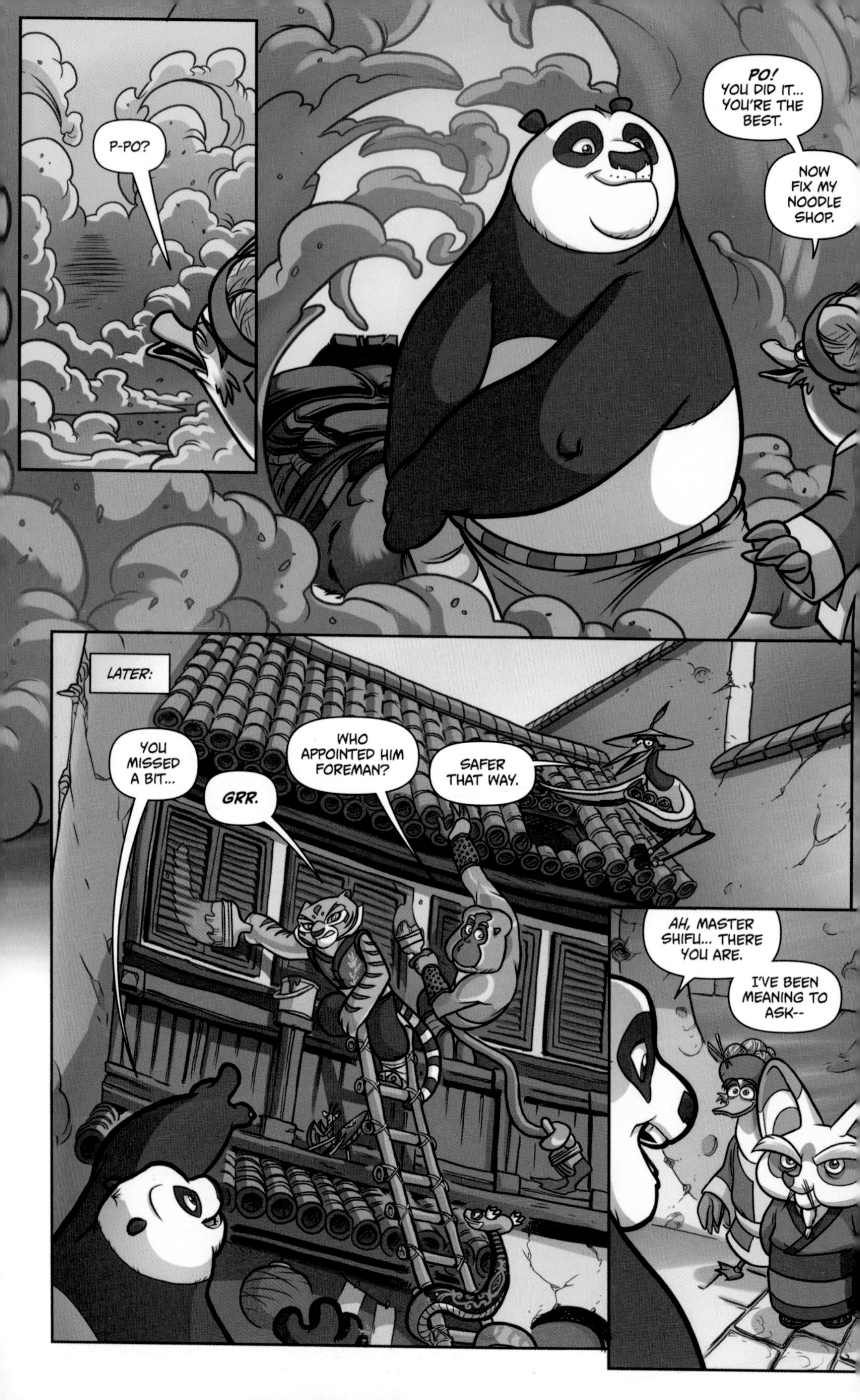
P-PO?
PO! YOU DID IT... YOU'RE THE BEST.
NOW FIX MY NOODLE SHOP.
LATER:
YOU MISSED A BIT...
GRR.
WHO APPOINTED HIM FOREMAN?
SAFER THAT WAY.
AH, MASTER SHIFU... THERE YOU ARE.
I'VE BEEN MEANING TO ASK--

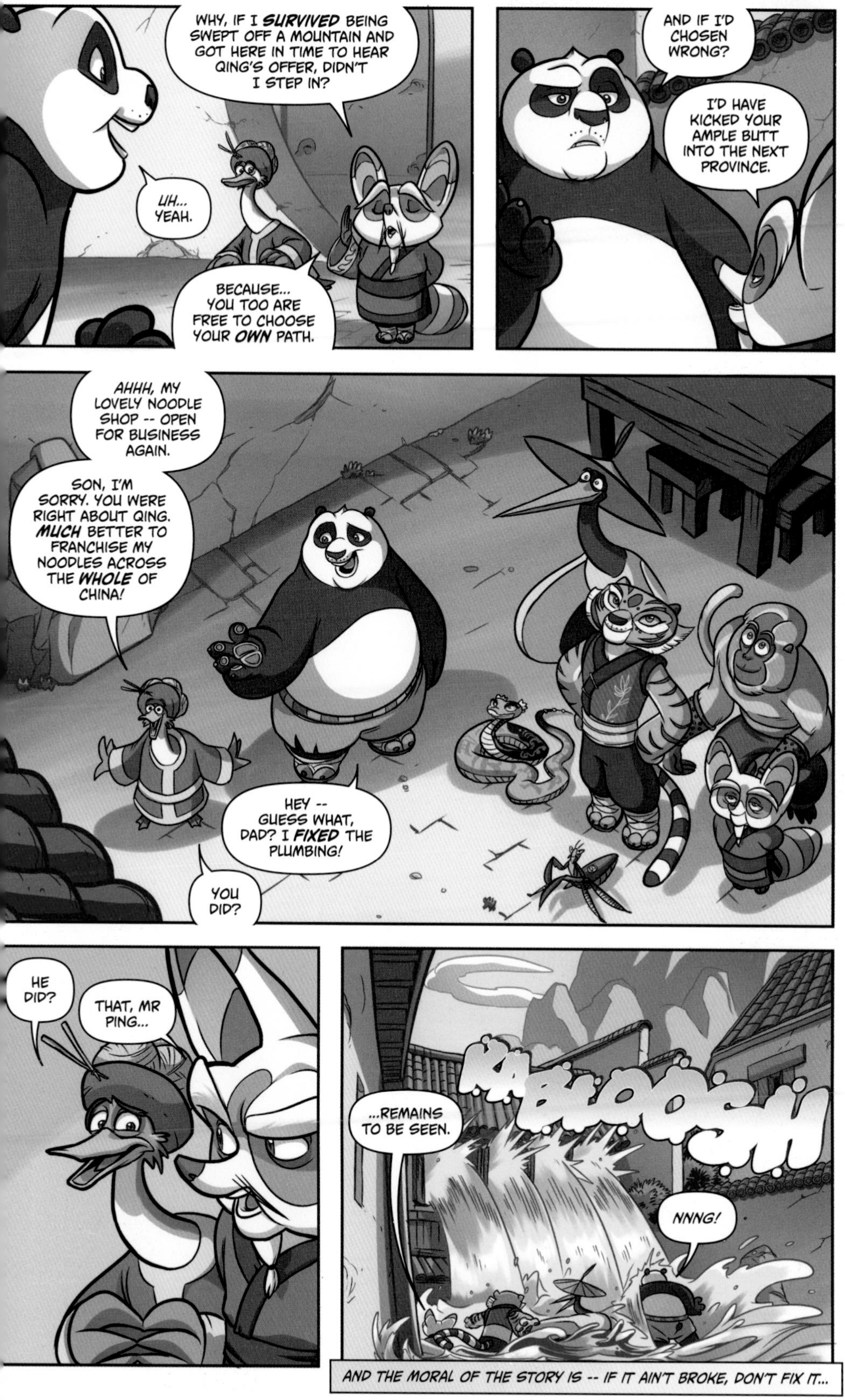
WHY, IF I SURVIVED BEING SWEPT OFF A MOUNTAIN AND GOT HERE IN TIME TO HEAR QING'S OFFER, DIDN'T I STEP IN?
UH... YEAH.
BECAUSE... YOU TOO ARE FREE TO CHOOSE YOUR OWN PATH.
AND IF I'D CHOSEN WRONG?
I'D HAVE KICKED YOUR AMPLE BUTT INTO THE NEXT PROVINCE.
AHHH, MY LOVELY NOODLE SHOP -- OPEN FOR BUSINESS AGAIN.
SON, I'M SORRY. YOU WERE RIGHT ABOUT QING. MUCH BETTER TO FRANCHISE MY NOODLES ACROSS THE WHOLE OF CHINA!
HEY -- GUESS WHAT, DAD? I FIXED THE PLUMBING!
YOU DID?
HE DID?
THAT, MR PING...
...REMAINS TO BE SEEN.
KA BLOOSH
NNNG!
AND THE MORAL OF THE STORY IS -- IF IT AIN'T BROKE, DON'T FIX IT...

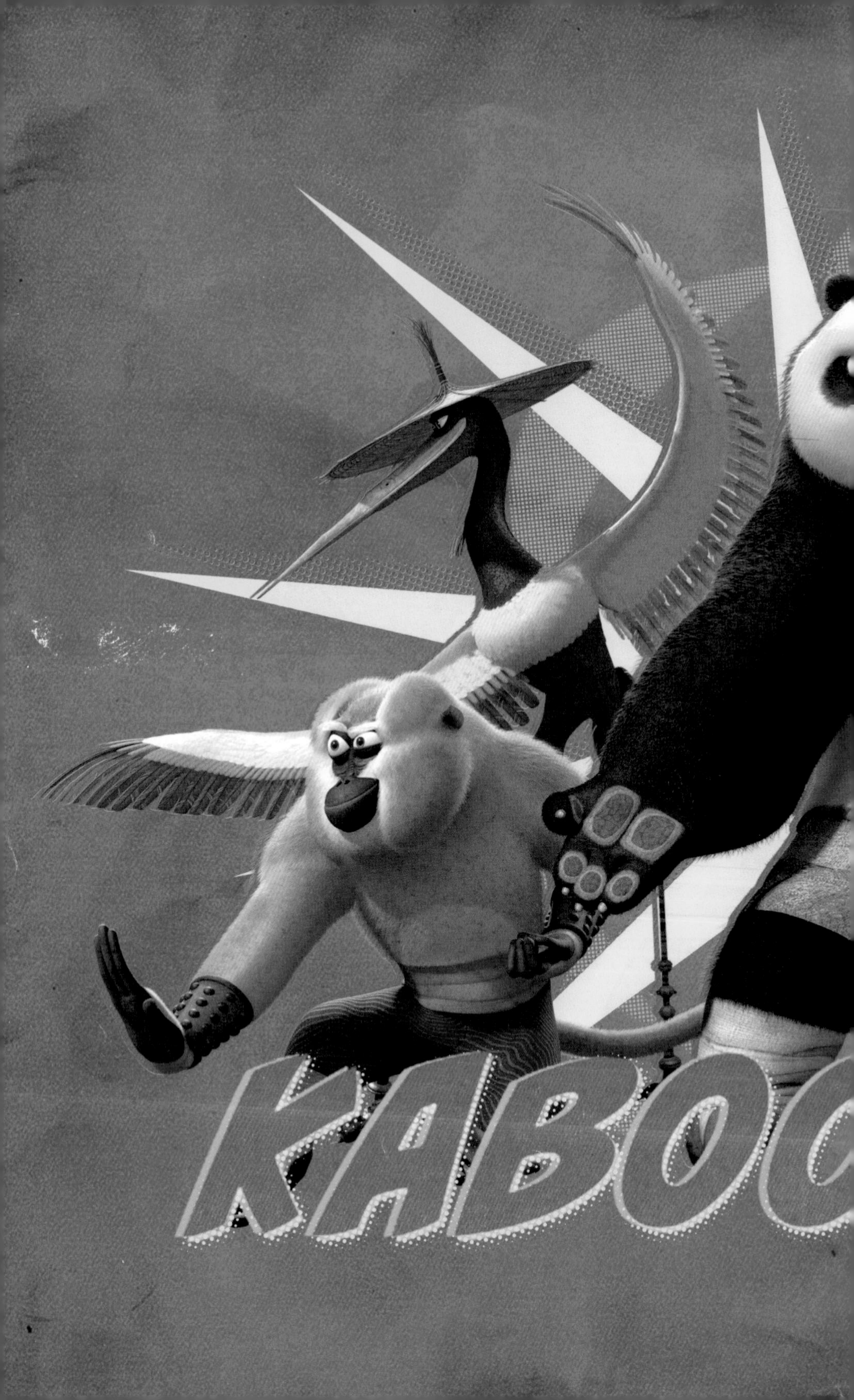
KABOO

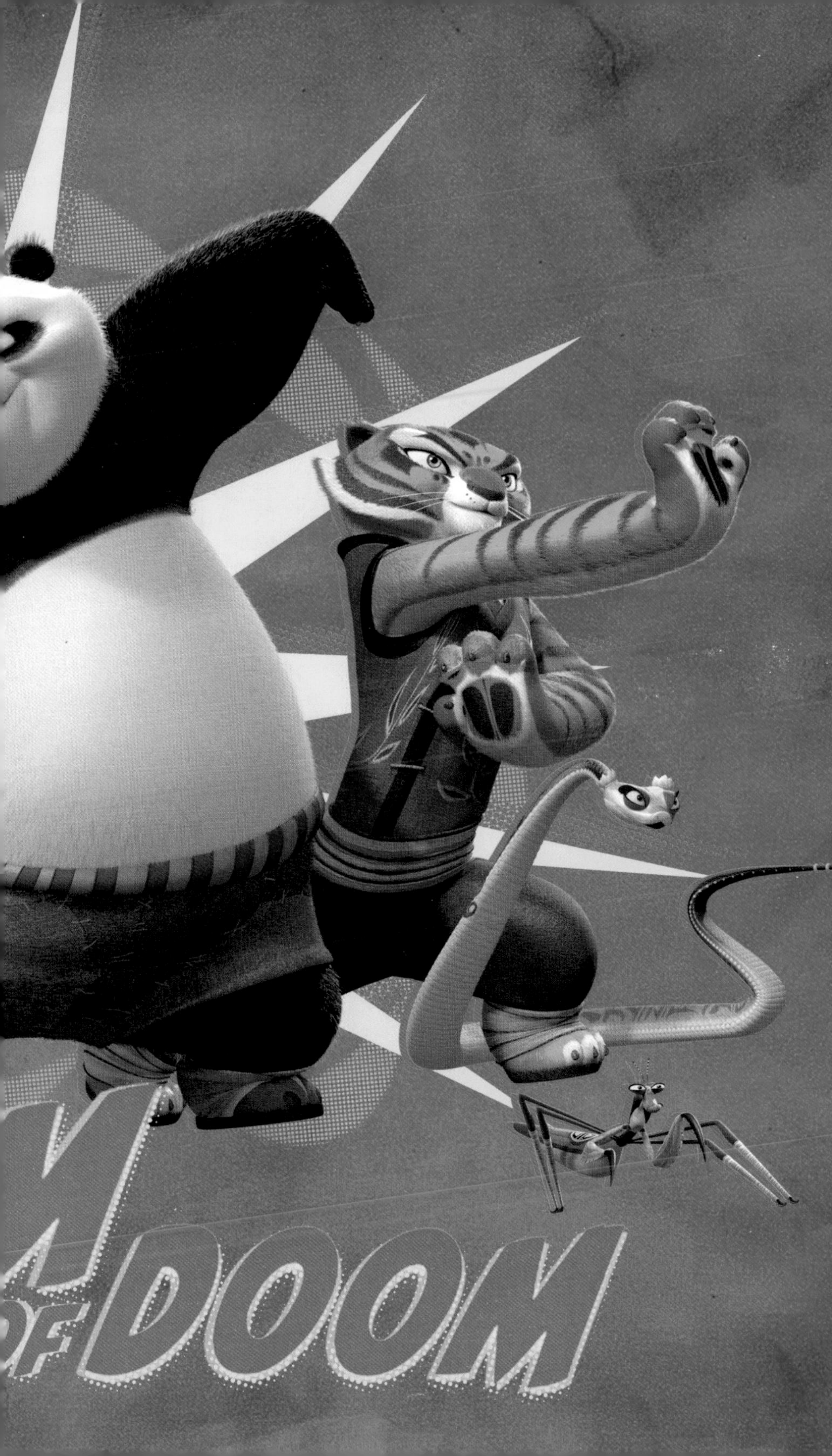
DOOM

DIVIDE & CONQUER

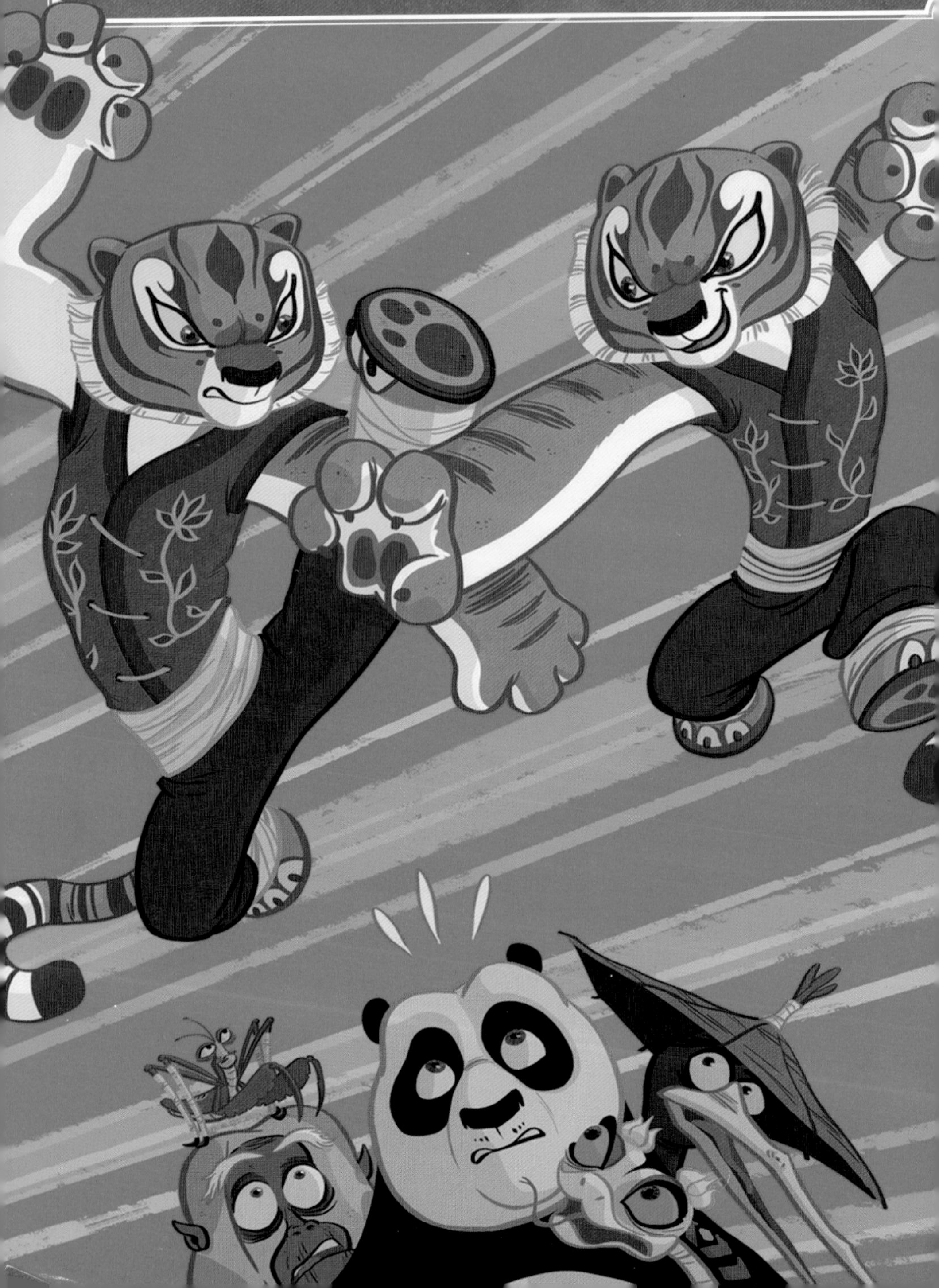

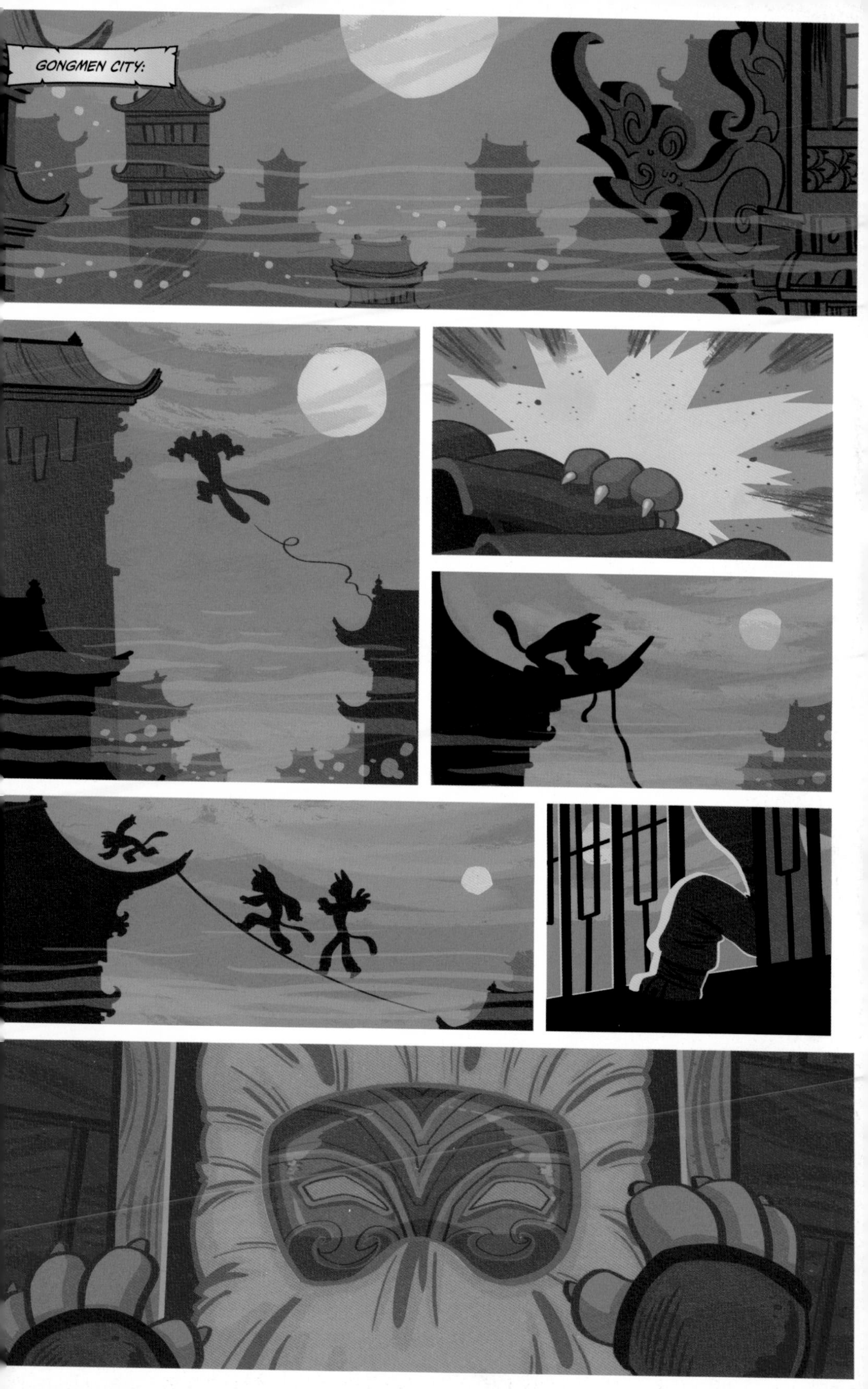
GONGMEN CITY:

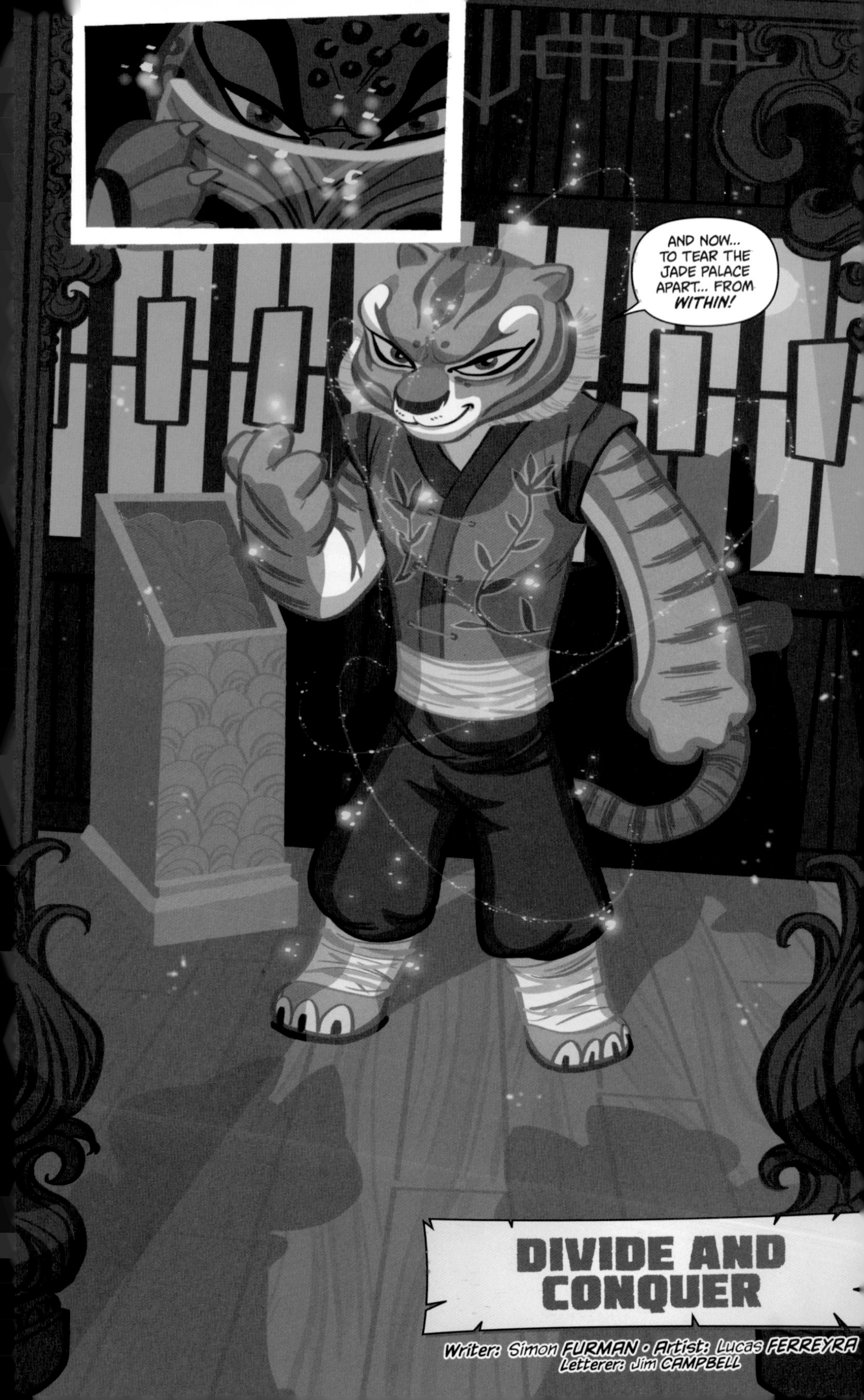
AND NOW... TO TEAR THE JADE PALACE APART... FROM *WITHIN!*
DIVIDE AND CONQUER
Writer: Simon FURMAN • Artist: Lucas FERREYRA
Letterer: Jim CAMPBELL

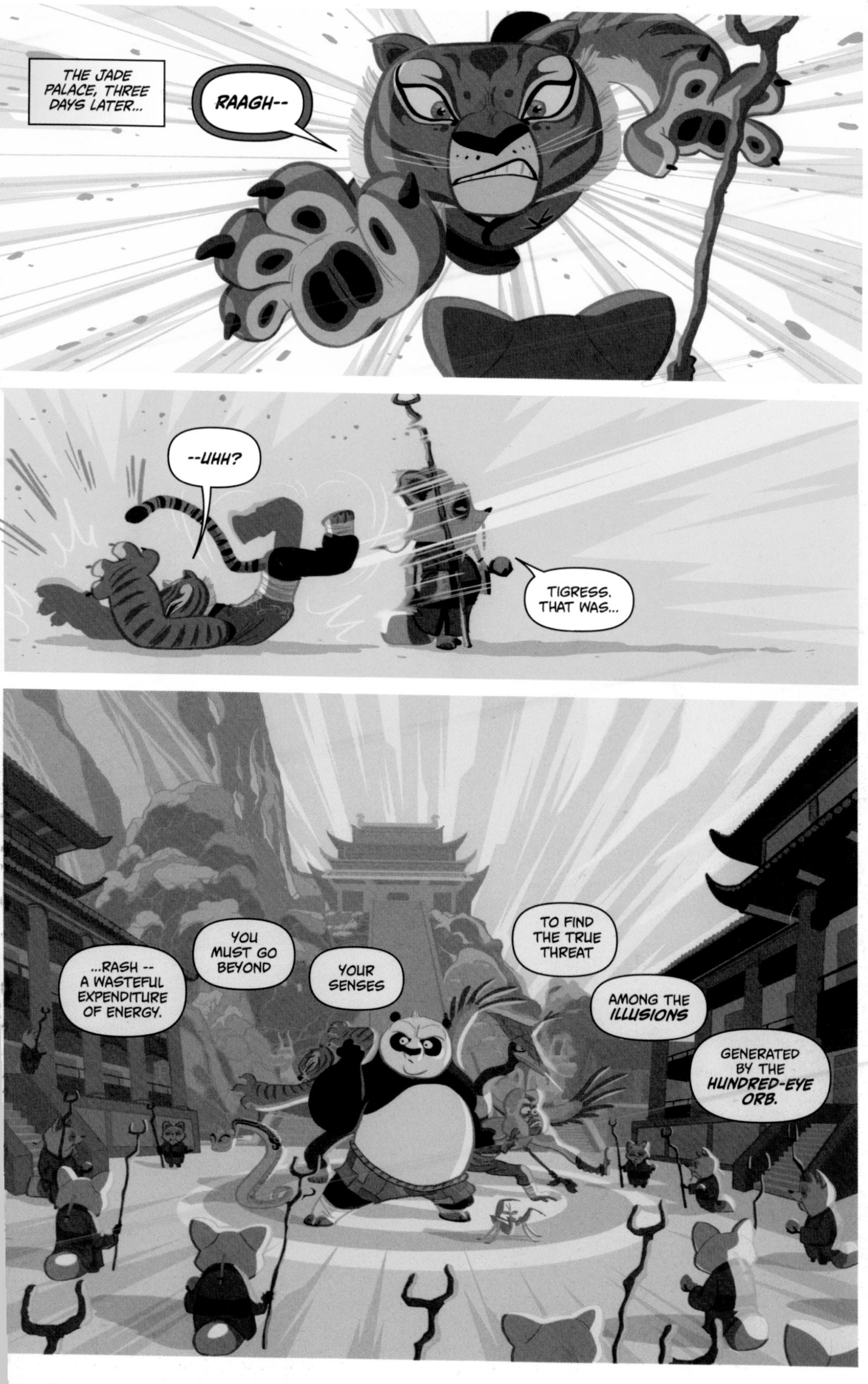
THE JADE PALACE, THREE DAYS LATER...
RAAGH--
--UHH?
TIGRESS. THAT WAS...
...RASH -- A WASTEFUL EXPENDITURE OF ENERGY.
YOU MUST GO BEYOND
YOUR SENSES
TO FIND THE TRUE THREAT
AMONG THE ILLUSIONS
GENERATED BY THE HUNDRED-EYE ORB.

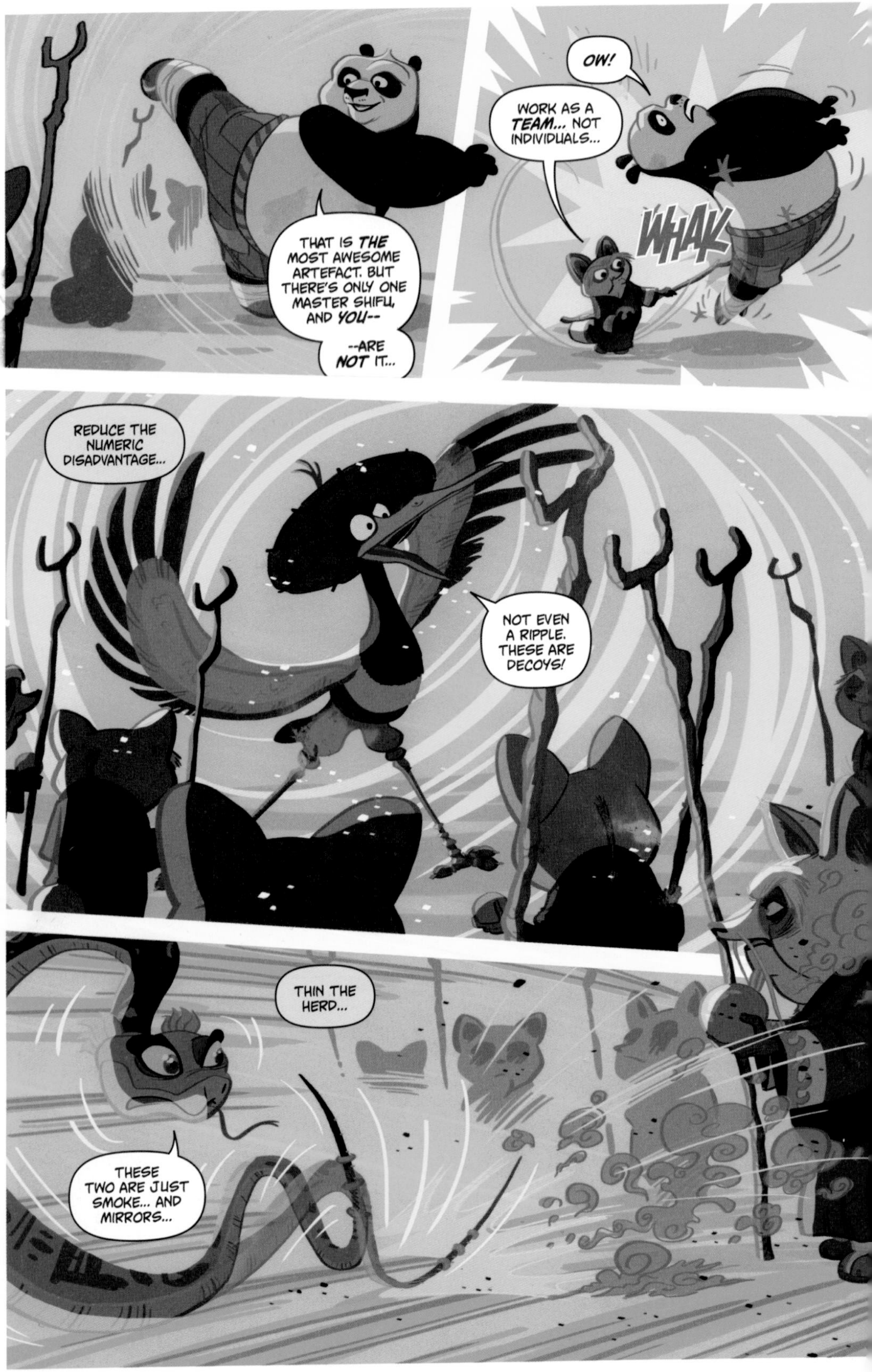
THAT IS THE MOST AWESOME ARTEFACT. BUT THERE'S ONLY ONE MASTER SHIFU, AND YOU--
--ARE NOT IT...
OW!
WORK AS A TEAM... NOT INDIVIDUALS...
WHAK
REDUCE THE NUMERIC DISADVANTAGE...
NOT EVEN A RIPPLE. THESE ARE DECOYS!
THIN THE HERD...
THESE TWO ARE JUST SMOKE... AND MIRRORS...

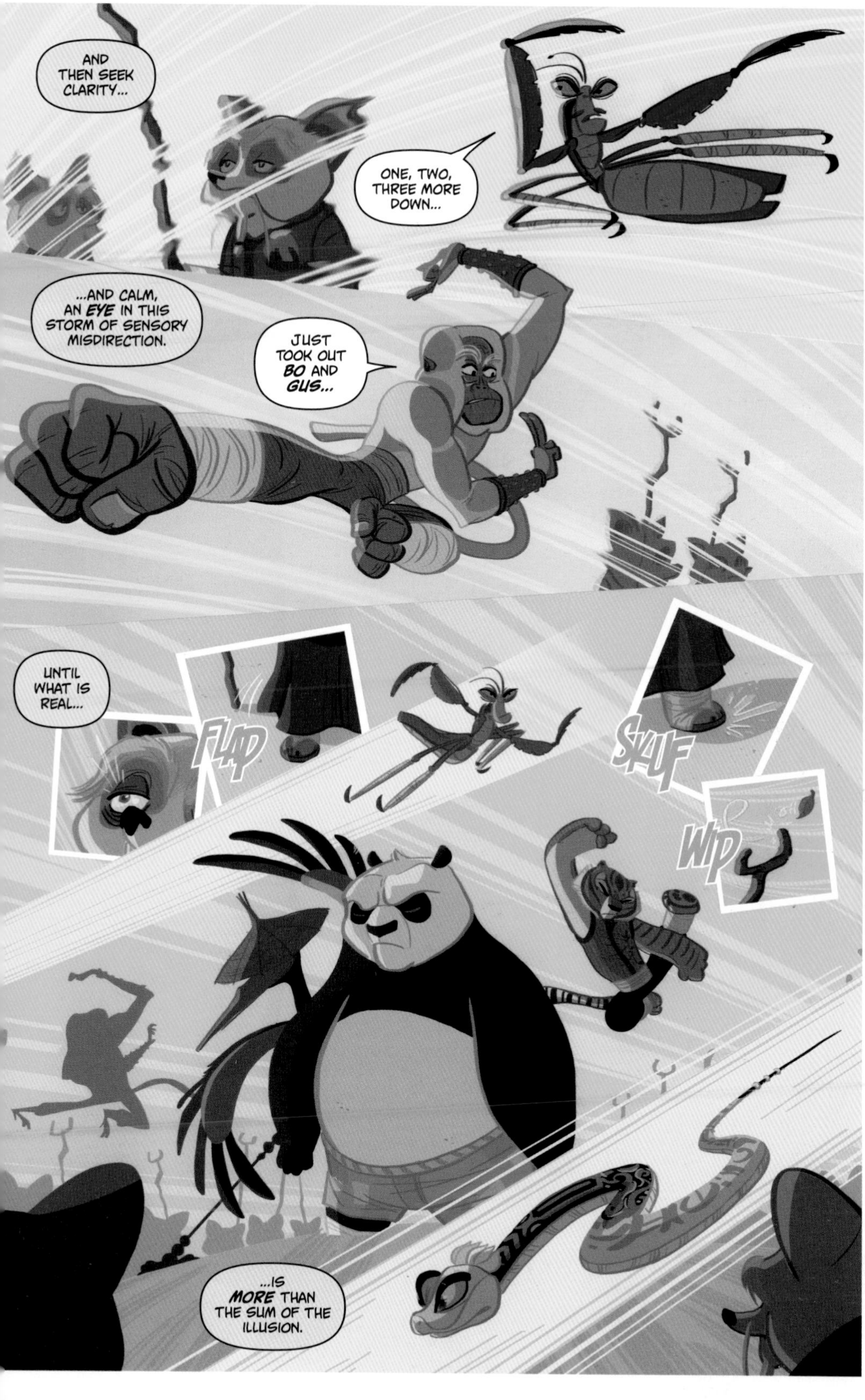
AND THEN SEEK CLARITY...
ONE, TWO, THREE MORE DOWN...
...AND CALM, AN EYE IN THIS STORM OF SENSORY MISDIRECTION.
JUST TOOK OUT BO AND GUS...
UNTIL WHAT IS REAL...
FLAP
SKUF
WIP
...IS MORE THAN THE SUM OF THE ILLUSION.

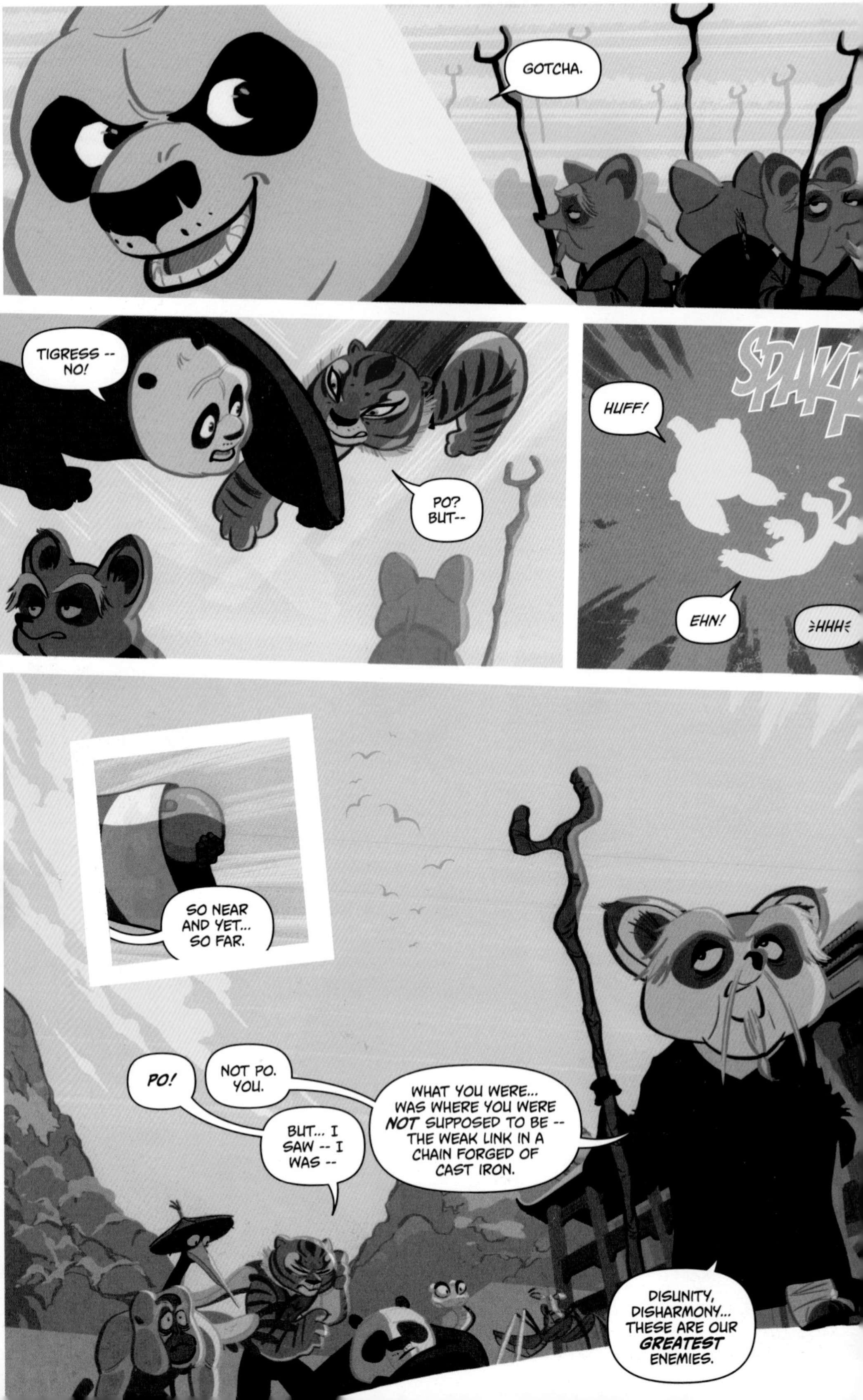
GOTCHA.
TIGRESS -- NO!
PO? BUT--
SPAK
HUFF!
EHN!
HHH
SO NEAR AND YET... SO FAR.
PO!
NOT PO. YOU.
BUT... I SAW -- I WAS --
WHAT YOU WERE... WAS WHERE YOU WERE NOT SUPPOSED TO BE -- THE WEAK LINK IN A CHAIN FORGED OF CAST IRON.
DISUNITY, DISHARMONY... THESE ARE OUR GREATEST ENEMIES.

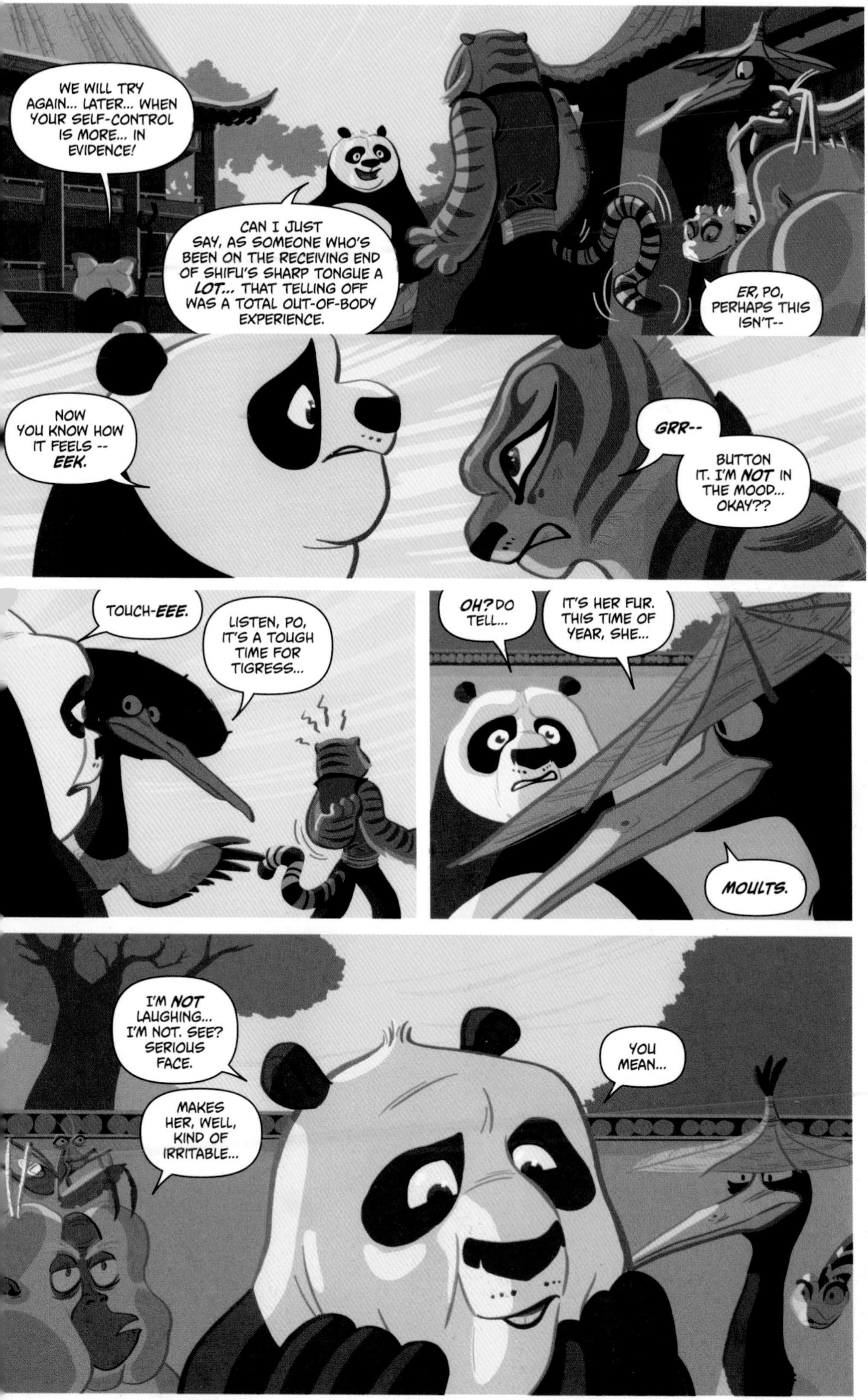
WE WILL TRY AGAIN... LATER... WHEN YOUR SELF-CONTROL IS MORE... IN EVIDENCE!
CAN I JUST SAY, AS SOMEONE WHO'S BEEN ON THE RECEIVING END OF SHIFU'S SHARP TONGUE A LOT... THAT TELLING OFF WAS A TOTAL OUT-OF-BODY EXPERIENCE.
ER, PO, PERHAPS THIS ISN'T--
NOW YOU KNOW HOW IT FEELS -- EEK.
GRR--
BUTTON IT. I'M NOT IN THE MOOD... OKAY??
TOUCH-EEE.
LISTEN, PO, IT'S A TOUGH TIME FOR TIGRESS...
OH? DO TELL...
IT'S HER FUR. THIS TIME OF YEAR, SHE...
MOULTS.
I'M NOT LAUGHING... I'M NOT. SEE? SERIOUS FACE.
MAKES HER, WELL, KIND OF IRRITABLE...
YOU MEAN...

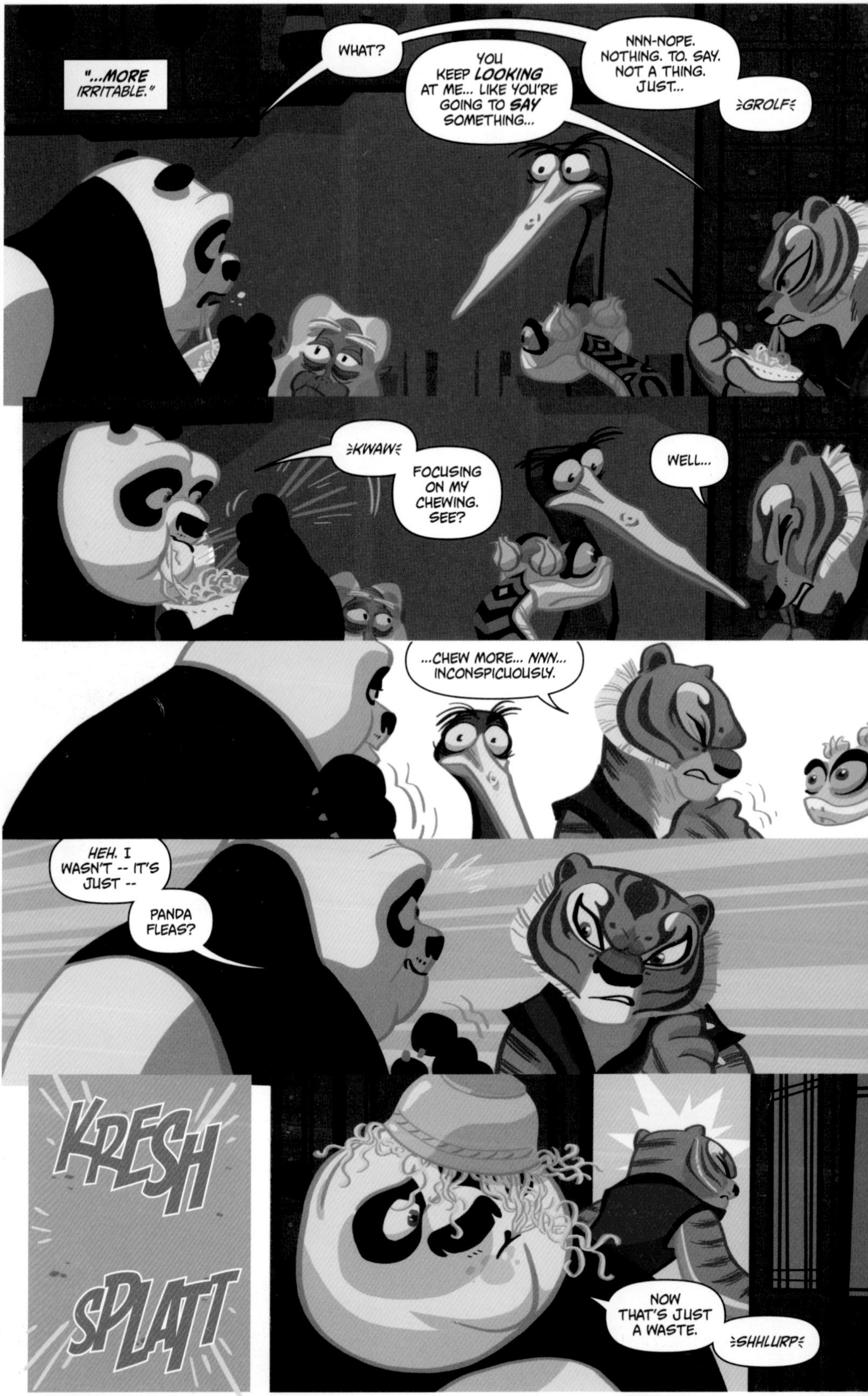
"...MORE IRRITABLE."
WHAT?
YOU KEEP LOOKING AT ME... LIKE YOU'RE GOING TO SAY SOMETHING...
NNN-NOPE. NOTHING. TO. SAY. NOT A THING. JUST...
GROLF
KWAW
FOCUSING ON MY CHEWING. SEE?
WELL...
...CHEW MORE... NNN... INCONSPICUOUSLY.
HEH. I WASN'T -- IT'S JUST --
PANDA FLEAS?
KRESH
SPLATT
NOW THAT'S JUST A WASTE.
SHHLURP

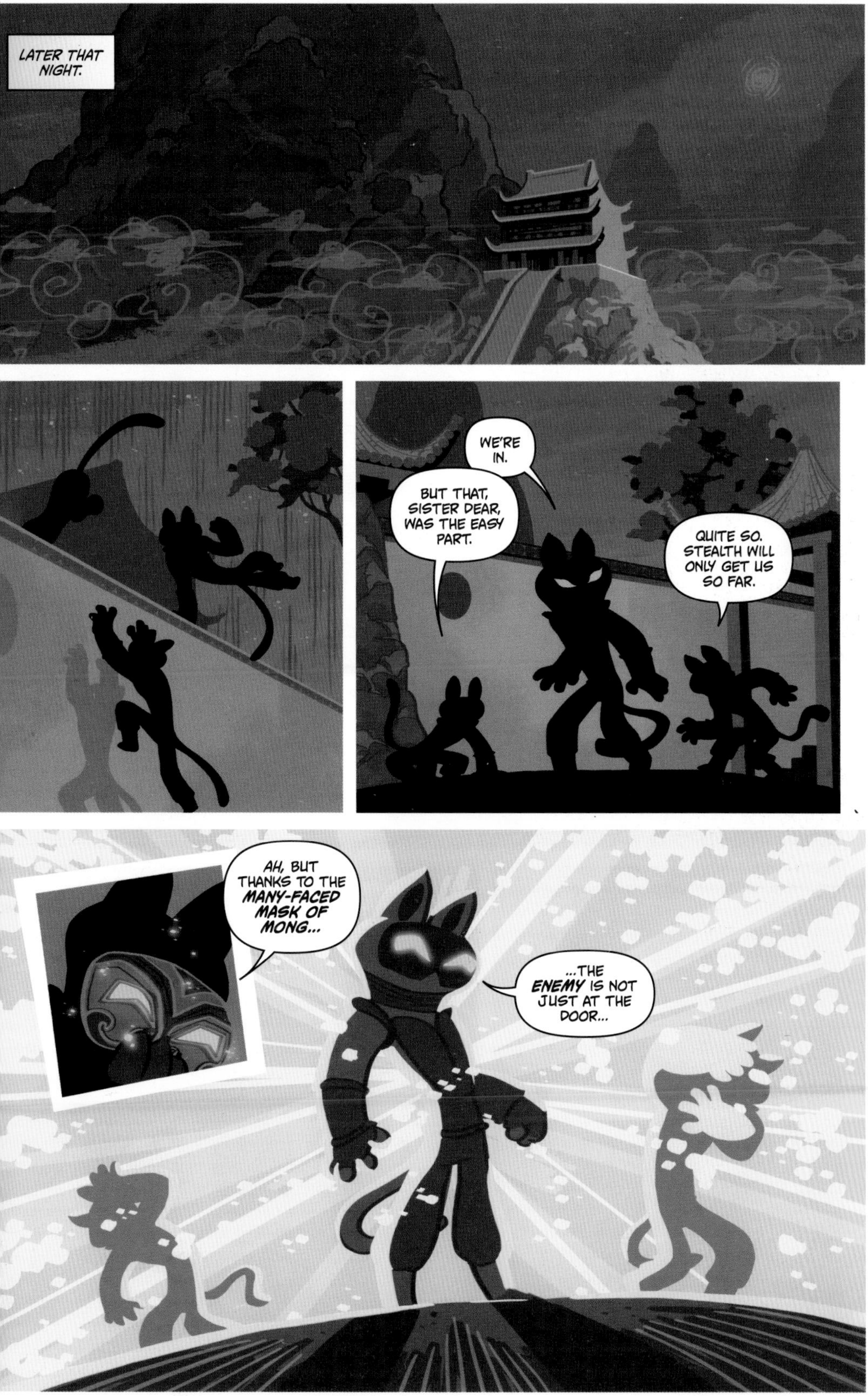
LATER THAT NIGHT.
WE'RE IN.
BUT THAT, SISTER DEAR, WAS THE EASY PART.
QUITE SO. STEALTH WILL ONLY GET US SO FAR.
AH, BUT THANKS TO THE MANY-FACED MASK OF MONG...
...THE ENEMY IS NOT JUST AT THE DOOR...

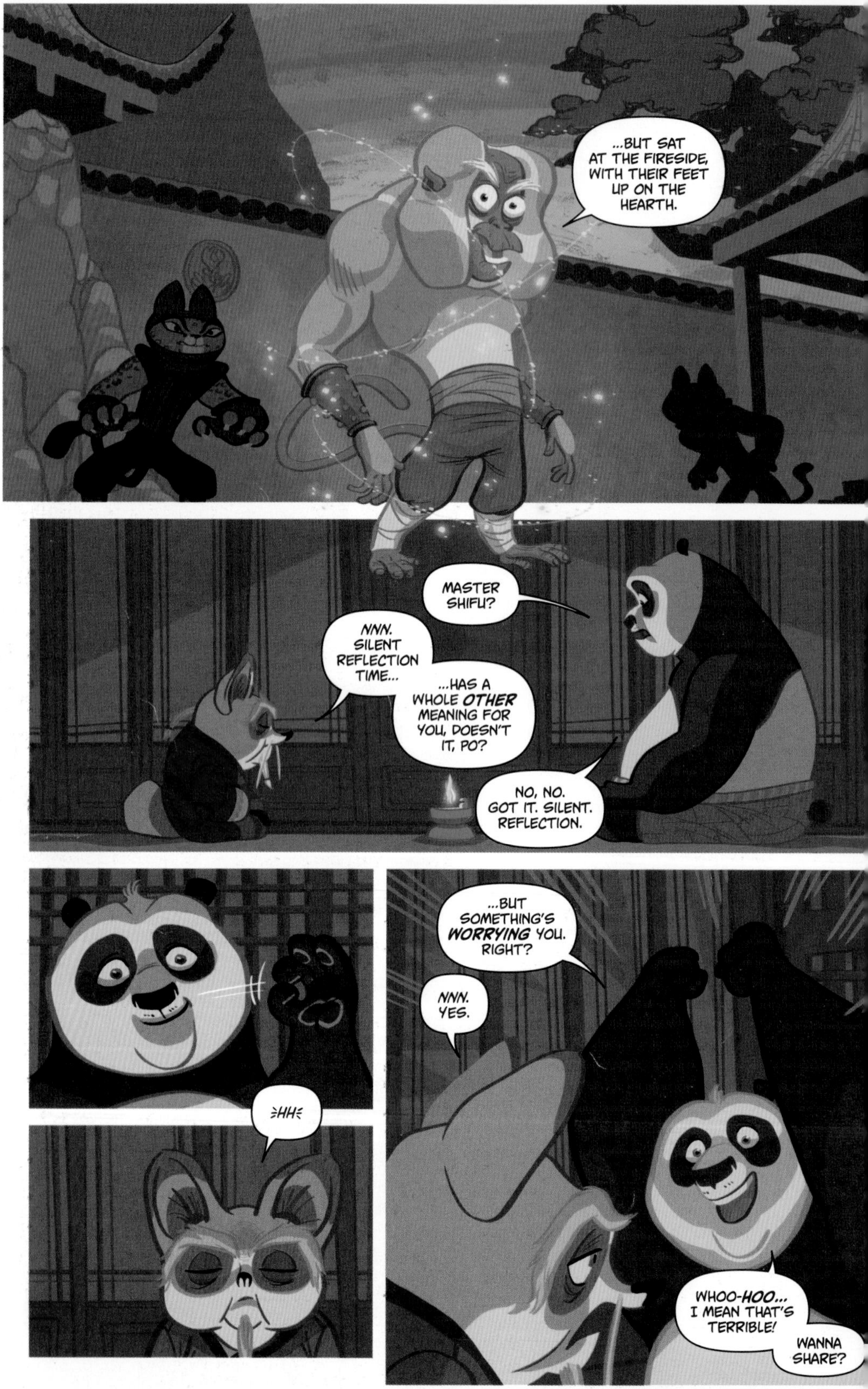
...BUT SAT AT THE FIRESIDE, WITH THEIR FEET UP ON THE HEARTH.
MASTER SHIFU?
NNN. SILENT REFLECTION TIME...
...HAS A WHOLE OTHER MEANING FOR YOU, DOESN'T IT, PO?
NO, NO. GOT IT. SILENT. REFLECTION.
HH
...BUT SOMETHING'S WORRYING YOU. RIGHT?
NNN. YES.
WHOO-HOO... I MEAN THAT'S TERRIBLE!
WANNA SHARE?

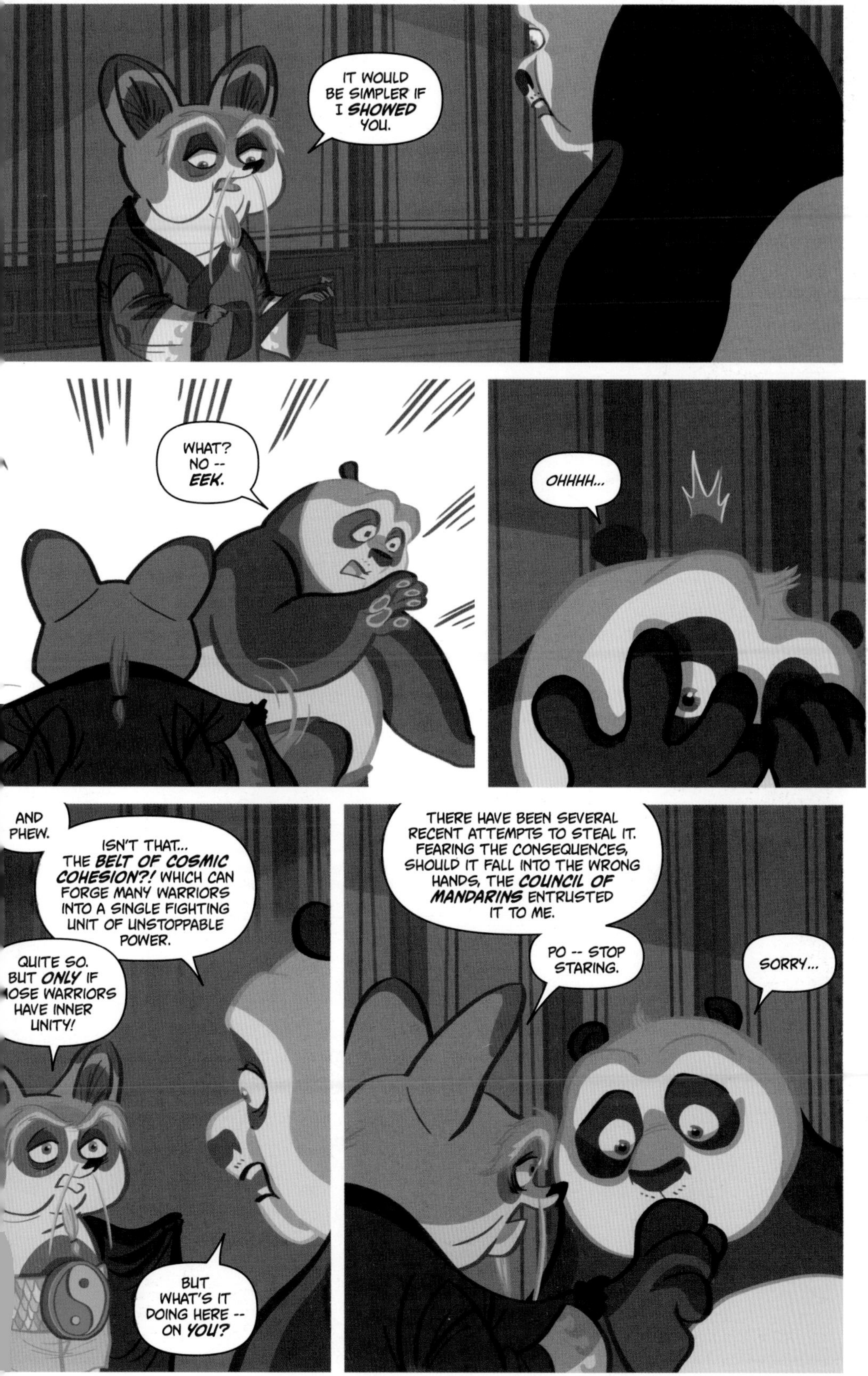

IT WOULD BE SIMPLER IF I SHOWED YOU.
WHAT? NO -- EEK.
OHHHH...
AND PHEW.
ISN'T THAT... THE BELT OF COSMIC COHESION?! WHICH CAN FORGE MANY WARRIORS INTO A SINGLE FIGHTING UNIT OF UNSTOPPABLE POWER.
QUITE SO. BUT ONLY IF OSE WARRIORS HAVE INNER UNITY!
BUT WHAT'S IT DOING HERE -- ON YOU?
THERE HAVE BEEN SEVERAL RECENT ATTEMPTS TO STEAL IT. FEARING THE CONSEQUENCES, SHOULD IT FALL INTO THE WRONG HANDS, THE COUNCIL OF MANDARINS ENTRUSTED IT TO ME.
PO -- STOP STARING.
SORRY...

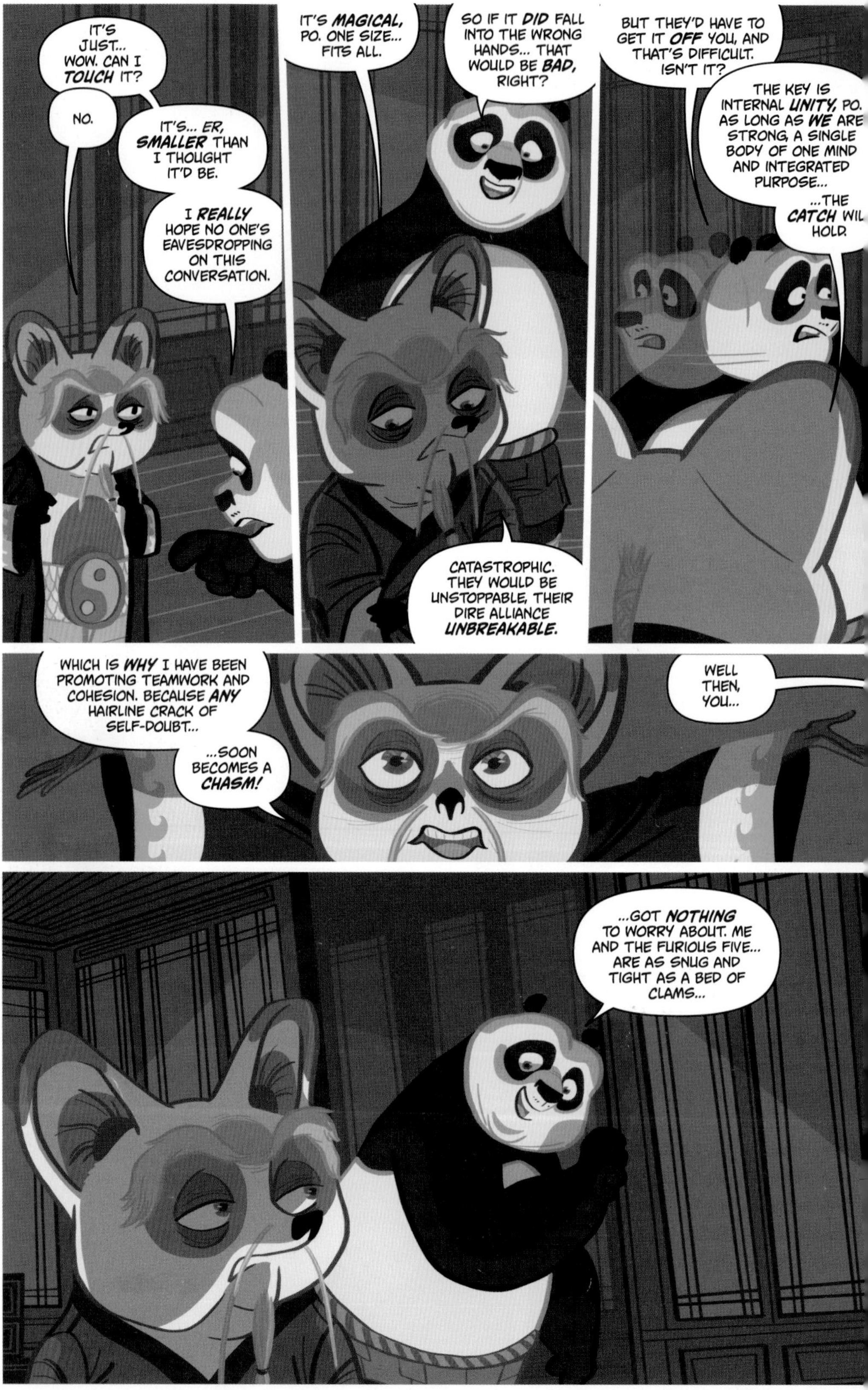

IT'S JUST... WOW. CAN I TOUCH IT?
NO.
IT'S... ER, SMALLER THAN I THOUGHT IT'D BE.
I REALLY HOPE NO ONE'S EAVESDROPPING ON THIS CONVERSATION.
IT'S MAGICAL, PO. ONE SIZE... FITS ALL.
SO IF IT DID FALL INTO THE WRONG HANDS... THAT WOULD BE BAD, RIGHT?
CATASTROPHIC. THEY WOULD BE UNSTOPPABLE, THEIR DIRE ALLIANCE UNBREAKABLE.
BUT THEY'D HAVE TO GET IT OFF YOU, AND THAT'S DIFFICULT. ISN'T IT?
THE KEY IS INTERNAL UNITY, PO. AS LONG AS WE ARE STRONG, A SINGLE BODY OF ONE MIND AND INTEGRATED PURPOSE...
...THE CATCH WIL HOLD.
WHICH IS WHY I HAVE BEEN PROMOTING TEAMWORK AND COHESION. BECAUSE ANY HAIRLINE CRACK OF SELF-DOUBT...
...SOON BECOMES A CHASM!
WELL THEN, YOU...
...GOT NOTHING TO WORRY ABOUT. ME AND THE FURIOUS FIVE... ARE AS SNUG AND TIGHT AS A BED OF CLAMS...

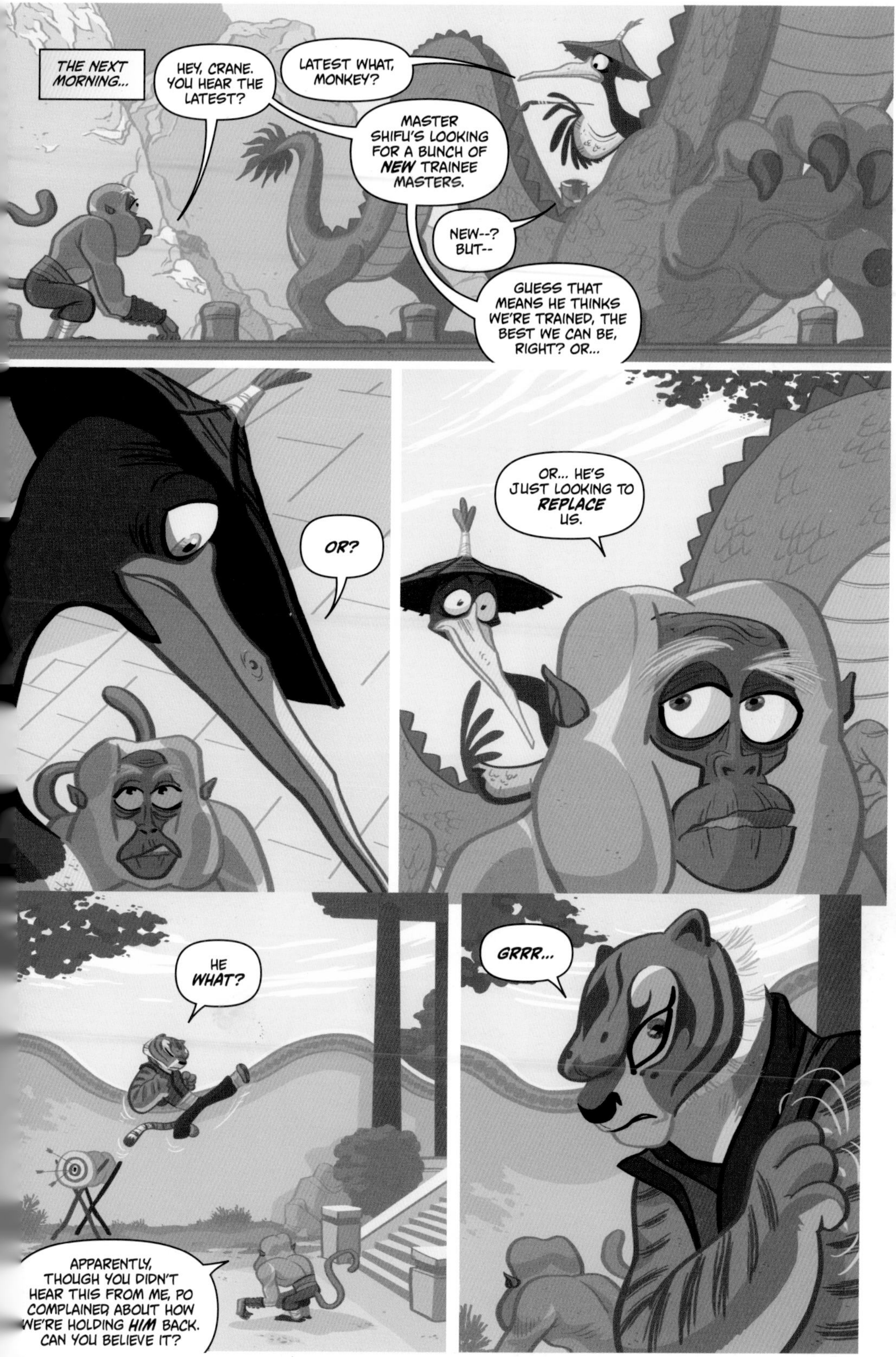
THE NEXT MORNING...
HEY, CRANE. YOU HEAR THE LATEST?
LATEST WHAT, MONKEY?
MASTER SHIFU'S LOOKING FOR A BUNCH OF NEW TRAINEE MASTERS.
NEW--? BUT--
GUESS THAT MEANS HE THINKS WE'RE TRAINED, THE BEST WE CAN BE, RIGHT? OR...
OR?
OR... HE'S JUST LOOKING TO REPLACE US.
HE WHAT?
APPARENTLY, THOUGH YOU DIDN'T HEAR THIS FROM ME, PO COMPLAINED ABOUT HOW WE'RE HOLDING HIM BACK. CAN YOU BELIEVE IT?
GRRR...

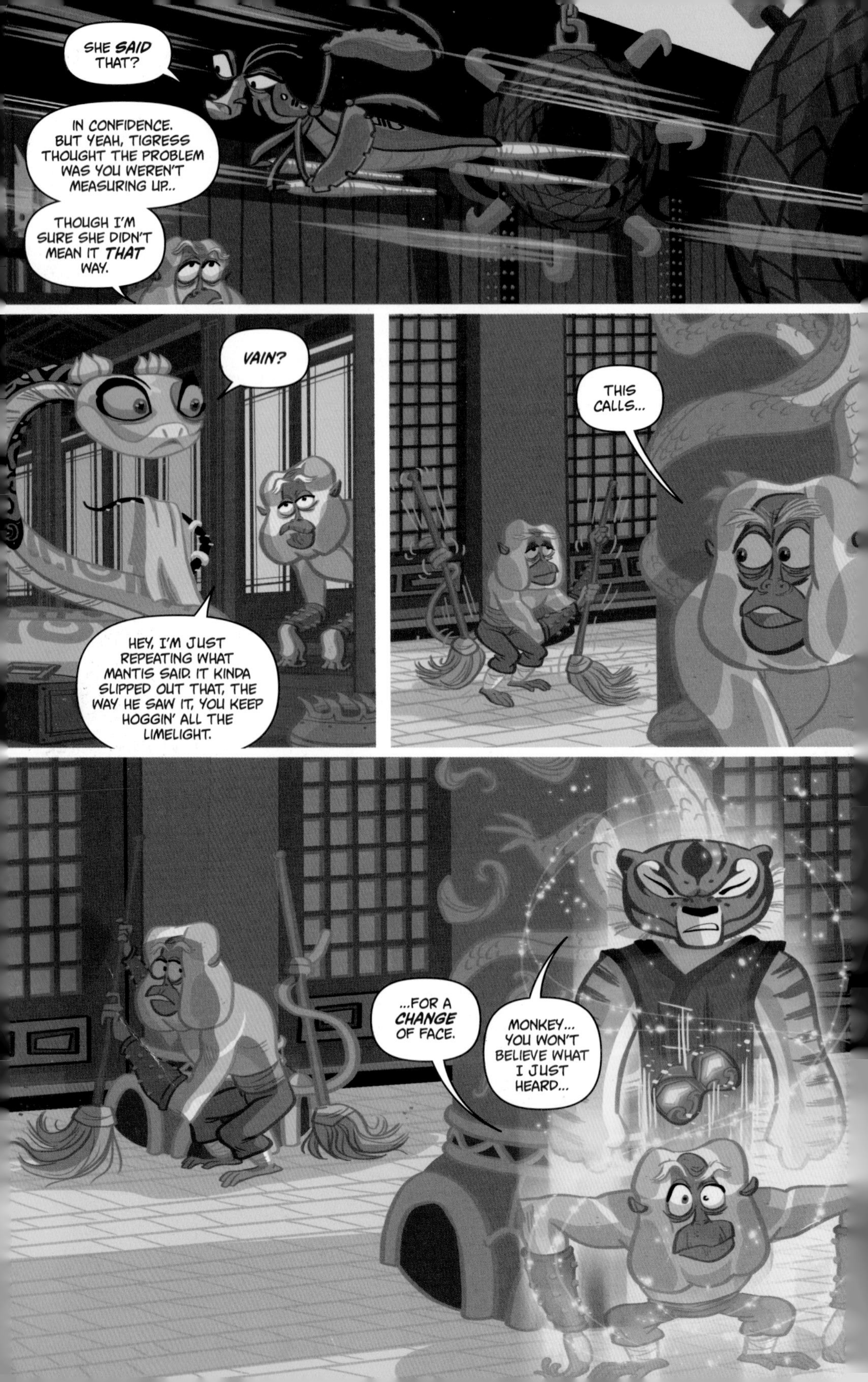
SHE SAID THAT?
IN CONFIDENCE. BUT YEAH, TIGRESS THOUGHT THE PROBLEM WAS YOU WEREN'T MEASURING UP...
THOUGH I'M SURE SHE DIDN'T MEAN IT THAT WAY.
VAIN?
HEY, I'M JUST REPEATING WHAT MANTIS SAID. IT KINDA SLIPPED OUT THAT, THE WAY HE SAW IT, YOU KEEP HOGGIN' ALL THE LIMELIGHT.
THIS CALLS...
...FOR A CHANGE OF FACE.
MONKEY... YOU WON'T BELIEVE WHAT I JUST HEARD...

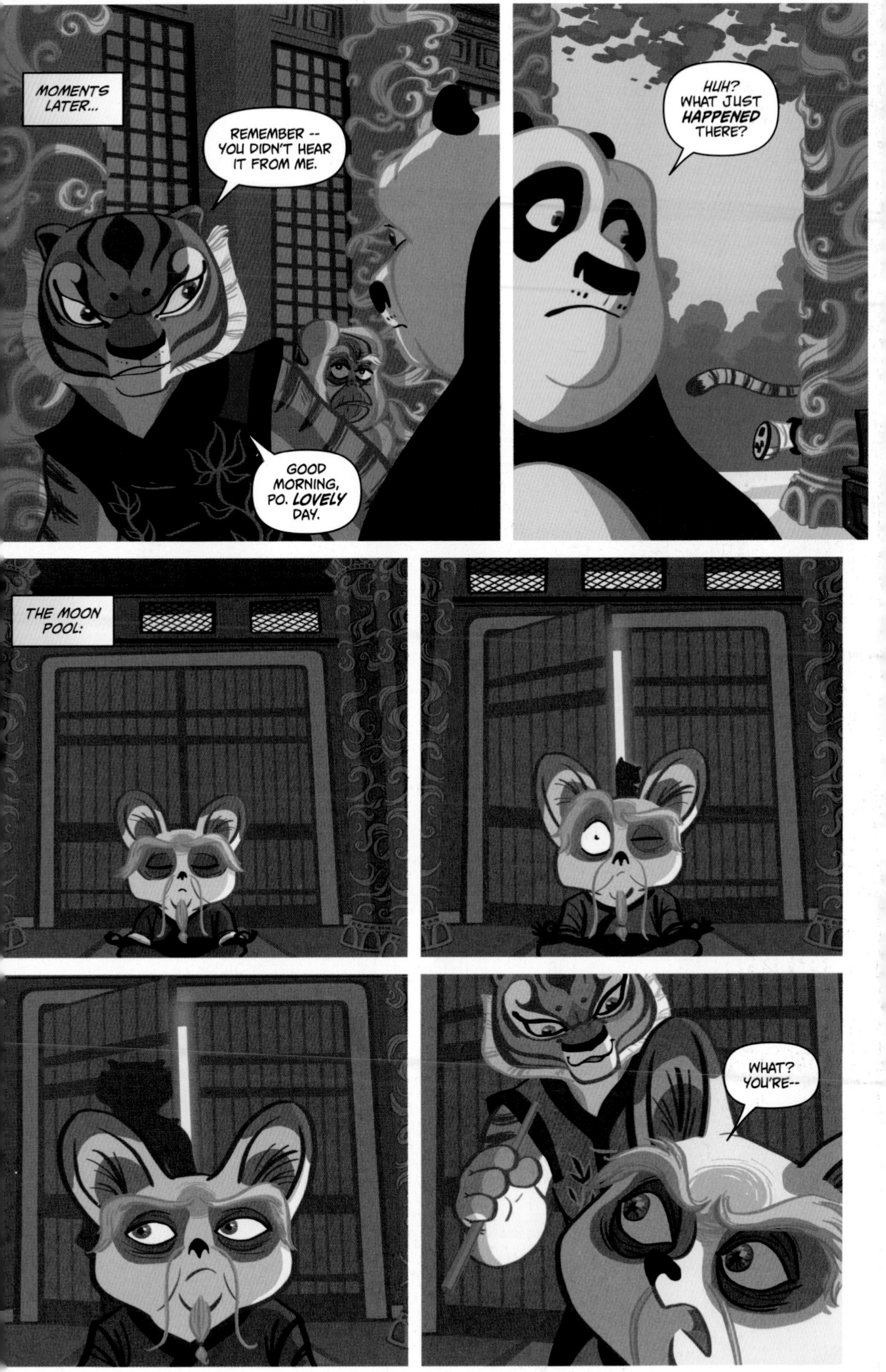
MOMENTS LATER...
REMEMBER -- YOU DIDN'T HEAR IT FROM ME.
GOOD MORNING, PO. LOVELY DAY.
HUH? WHAT JUST HAPPENED THERE?
THE MOON POOL:
WHAT? YOU'RE--

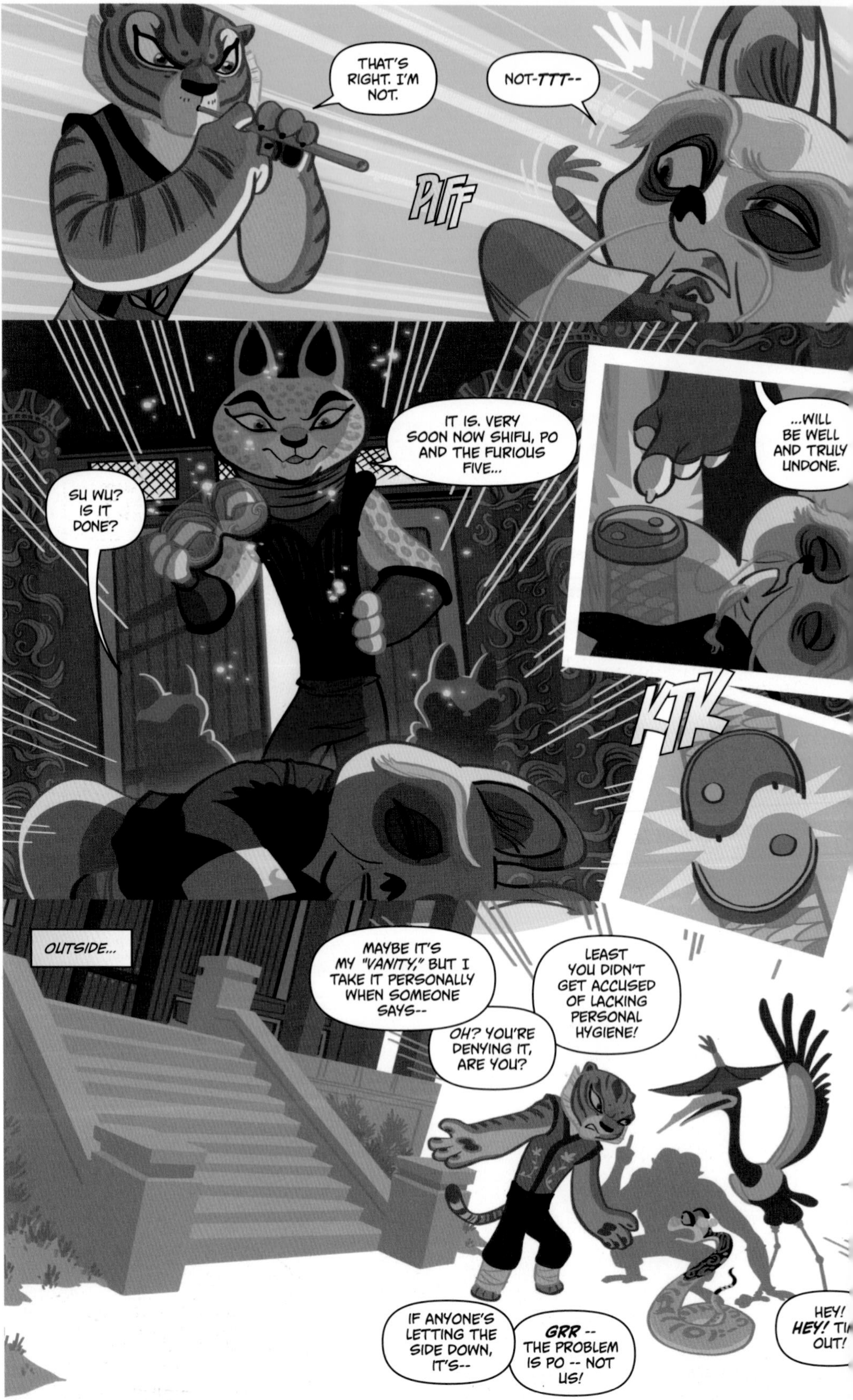
THAT'S RIGHT. I'M NOT.
NOT-TTT--
PIFF
SU WU? IS IT DONE?
IT IS. VERY SOON NOW SHIFU, PO AND THE FURIOUS FIVE...
...WILL BE WELL AND TRULY UNDONE.
KTK
OUTSIDE...
MAYBE IT'S MY "VANITY," BUT I TAKE IT PERSONALLY WHEN SOMEONE SAYS--
OH? YOU'RE DENYING IT, ARE YOU?
LEAST YOU DIDN'T GET ACCUSED OF LACKING PERSONAL HYGIENE!
IF ANYONE'S LETTING THE SIDE DOWN, IT'S--
GRR -- THE PROBLEM IS PO -- NOT US!
HEY! HEY! TI OUT!

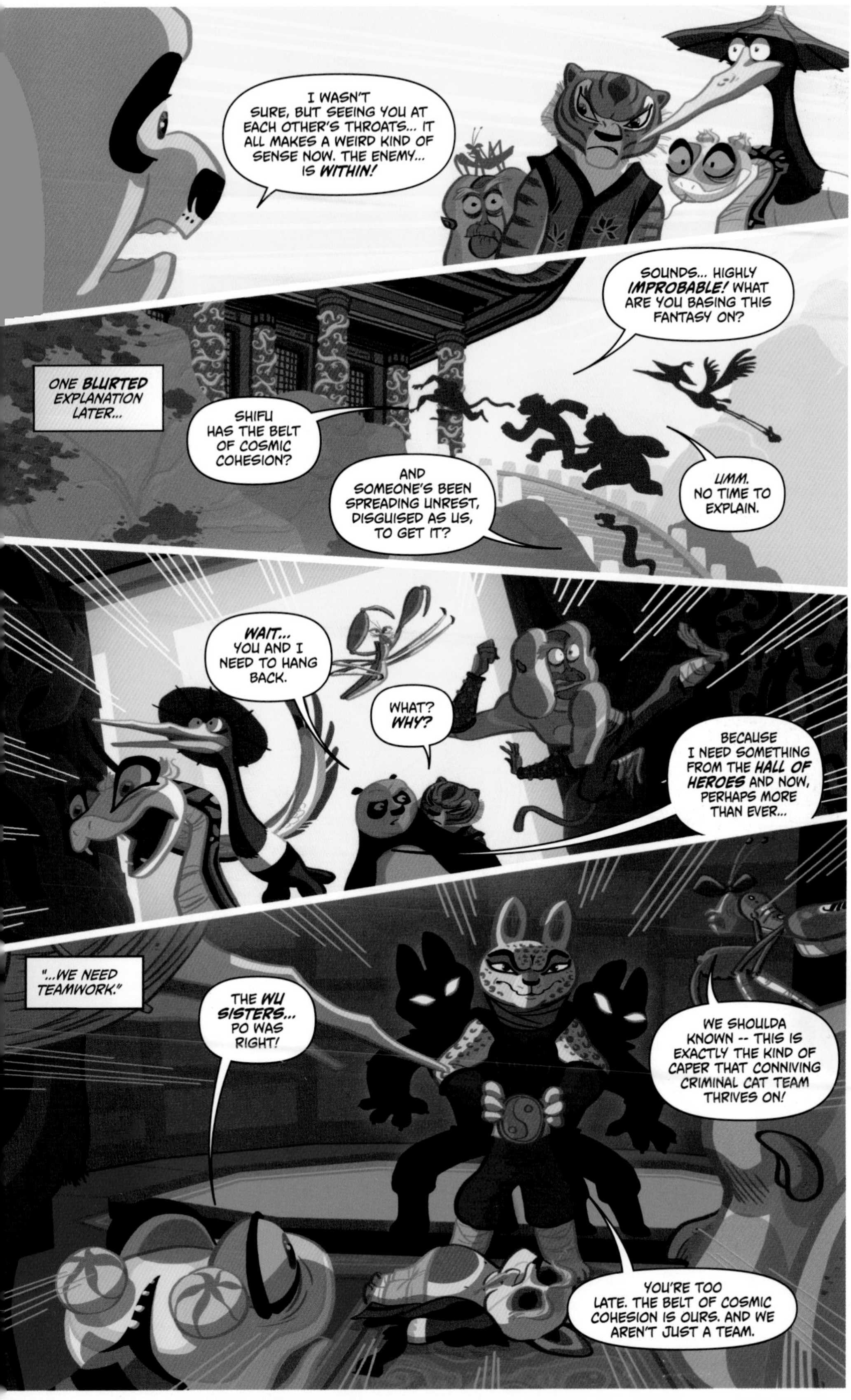
I WASN'T SURE, BUT SEEING YOU AT EACH OTHER'S THROATS... IT ALL MAKES A WEIRD KIND OF SENSE NOW. THE ENEMY... IS WITHIN!
SOUNDS... HIGHLY IMPROBABLE! WHAT ARE YOU BASING THIS FANTASY ON?
ONE BLURTED EXPLANATION LATER...
SHIFU HAS THE BELT OF COSMIC COHESION?
AND SOMEONE'S BEEN SPREADING UNREST, DISGUISED AS US, TO GET IT?
UMM. NO TIME TO EXPLAIN.
WAIT... YOU AND I NEED TO HANG BACK.
WHAT? WHY?
BECAUSE I NEED SOMETHING FROM THE HALL OF HEROES AND NOW, PERHAPS MORE THAN EVER...
"...WE NEED TEAMWORK."
THE WU SISTERS... PO WAS RIGHT!
WE SHOULDA KNOWN -- THIS IS EXACTLY THE KIND OF CAPER THAT CONNIVING CRIMINAL CAT TEAM THRIVES ON!
YOU'RE TOO LATE. THE BELT OF COSMIC COHESION IS OURS. AND WE AREN'T JUST A TEAM.

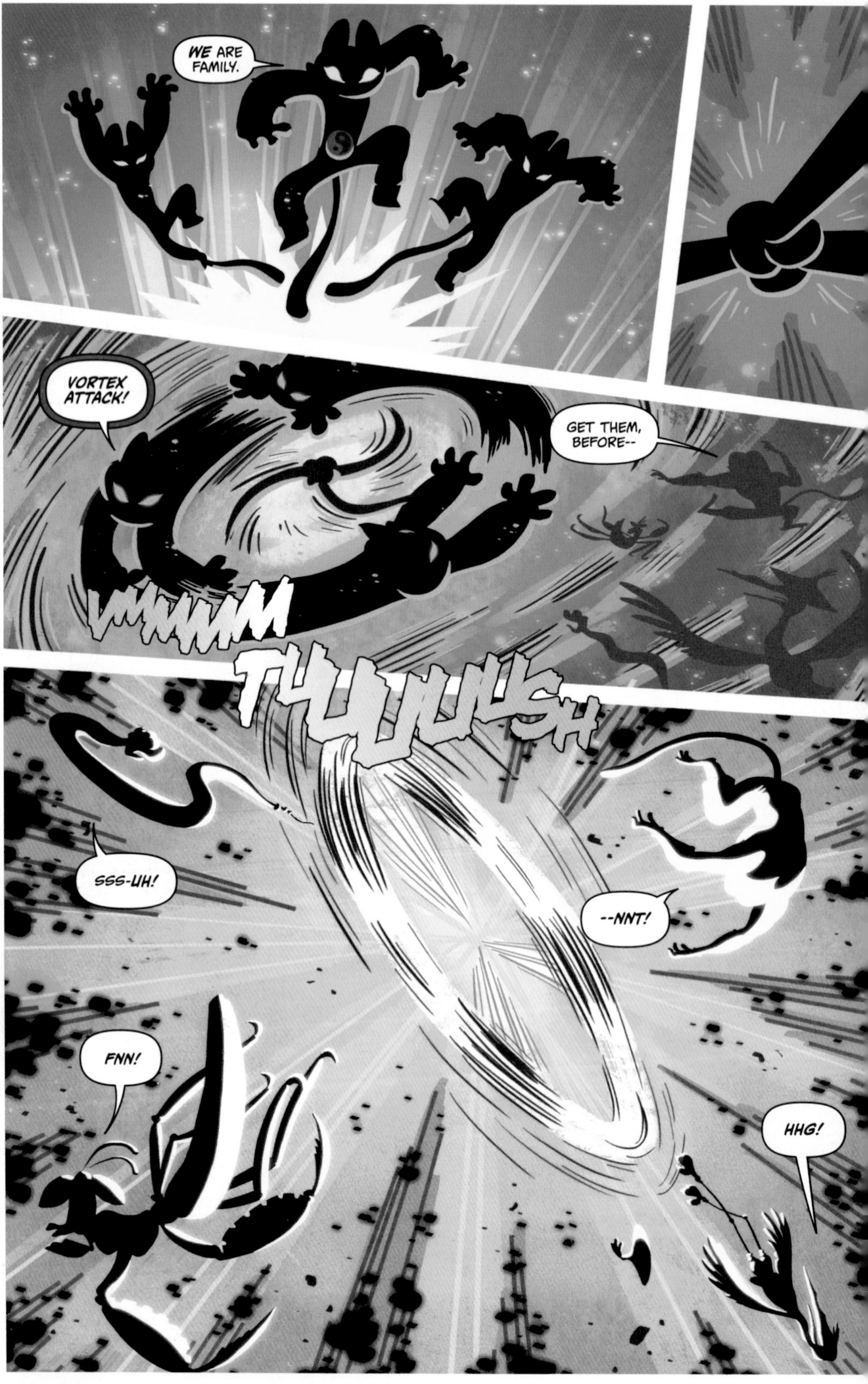
WE ARE FAMILY.
VORTEX ATTACK!
GET THEM, BEFORE--
VMMMM
TYUUUUSH
SSS-UH!
--NNT!
FNN!
HHG!

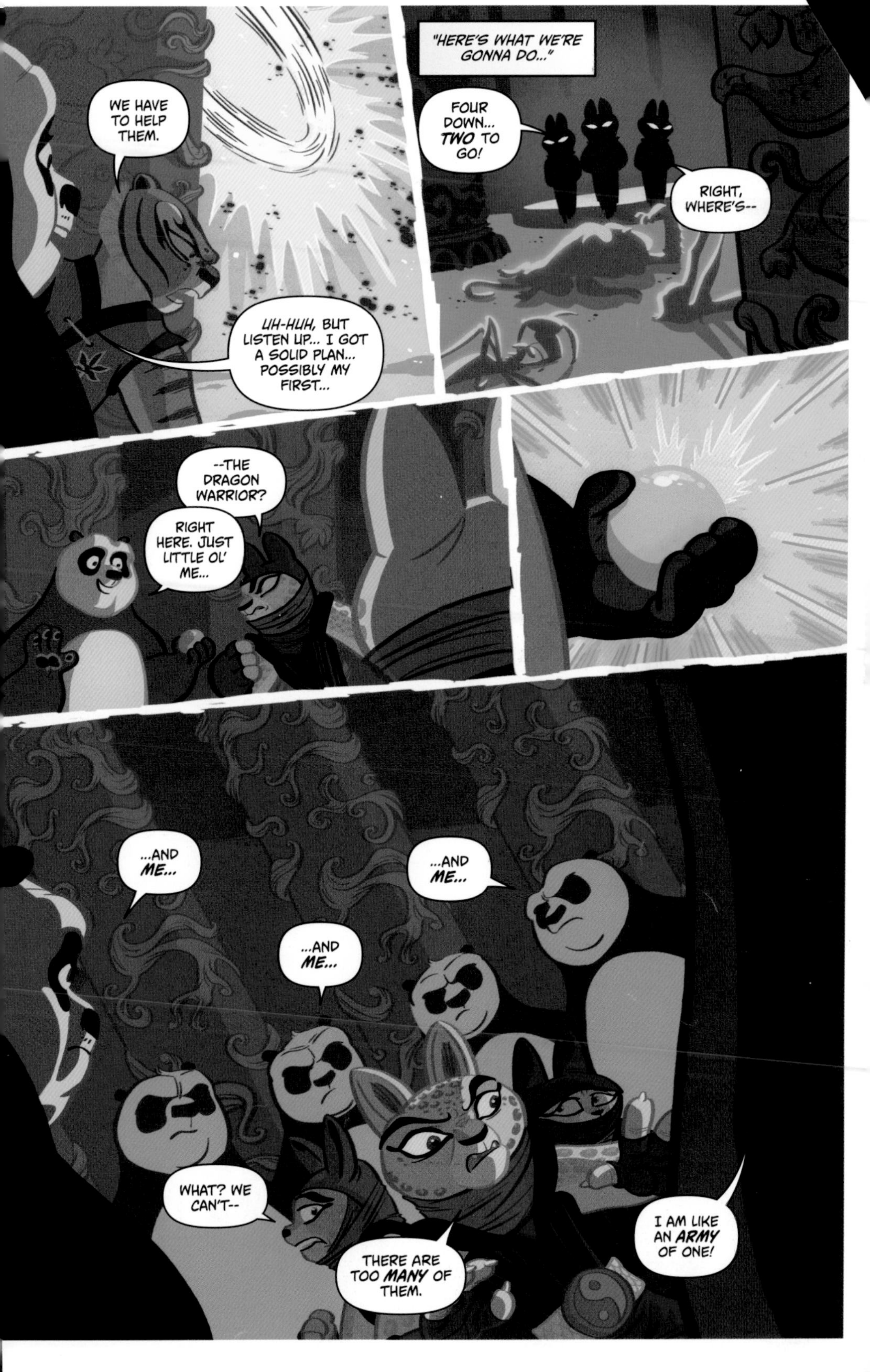
WE HAVE TO HELP THEM.
UH-HUH, BUT LISTEN UP... I GOT A SOLID PLAN... POSSIBLY MY FIRST...
"HERE'S WHAT WE'RE GONNA DO..."
FOUR DOWN... TWO TO GO!
RIGHT, WHERE'S--
--THE DRAGON WARRIOR?
RIGHT HERE. JUST LITTLE OL' ME...
...AND ME...
...AND ME...
...AND ME...
WHAT? WE CAN'T--
THERE ARE TOO MANY OF THEM.
I AM LIKE AN ARMY OF ONE!

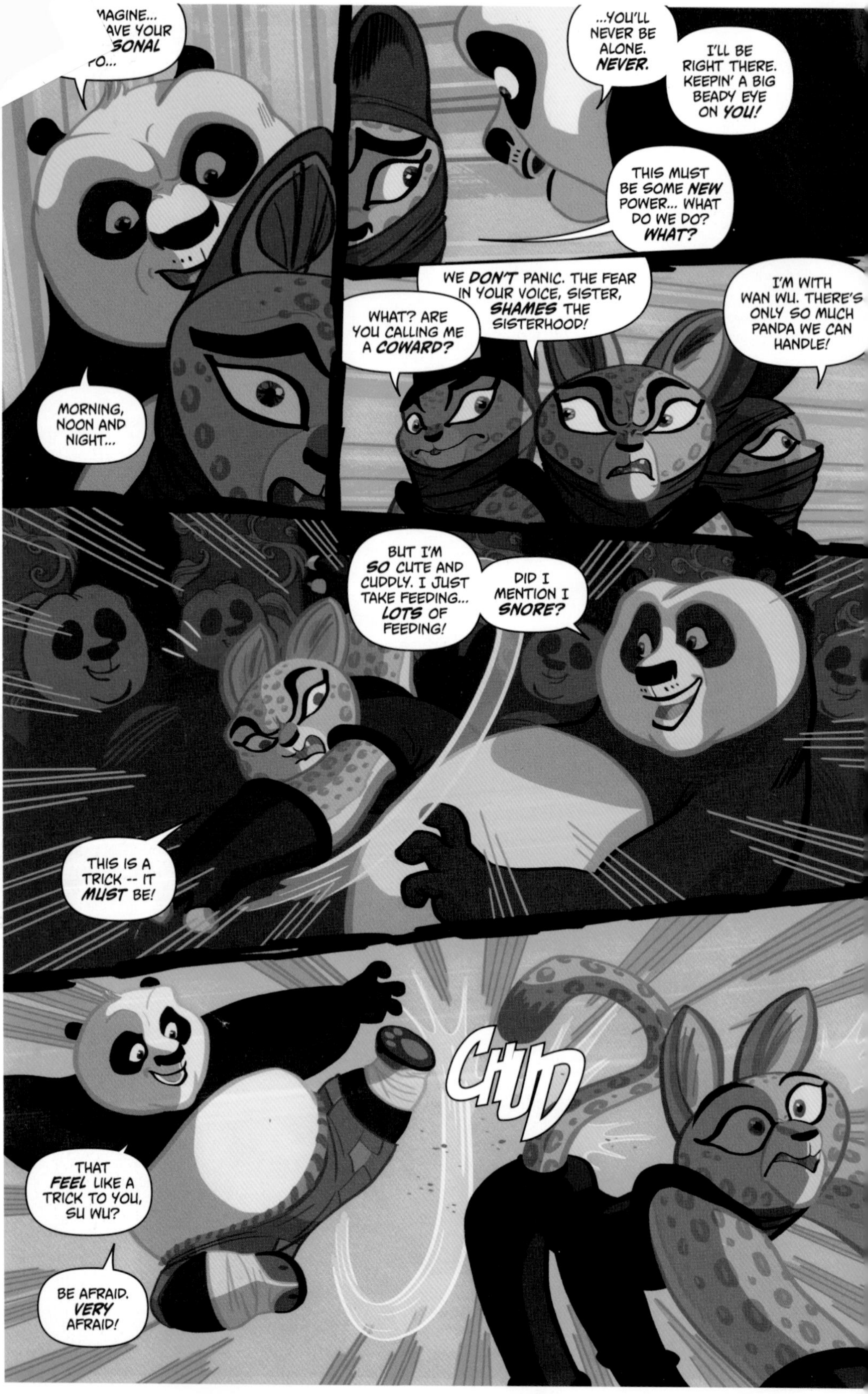

MAGINE... AVE YOUR SONAL O...
...YOU'LL NEVER BE ALONE. NEVER.
I'LL BE RIGHT THERE. KEEPIN' A BIG BEADY EYE ON YOU!
THIS MUST BE SOME NEW POWER... WHAT DO WE DO? WHAT?
MORNING, NOON AND NIGHT...
WHAT? ARE YOU CALLING ME A COWARD?
WE DON'T PANIC. THE FEAR IN YOUR VOICE, SISTER, SHAMES THE SISTERHOOD!
I'M WITH WAN WU. THERE'S ONLY SO MUCH PANDA WE CAN HANDLE!
BUT I'M SO CUTE AND CUDDLY. I JUST TAKE FEEDING... LOTS OF FEEDING!
DID I MENTION I SNORE?
THIS IS A TRICK -- IT MUST BE!
CHUD
THAT FEEL LIKE A TRICK TO YOU, SU WU?
BE AFRAID. VERY AFRAID!

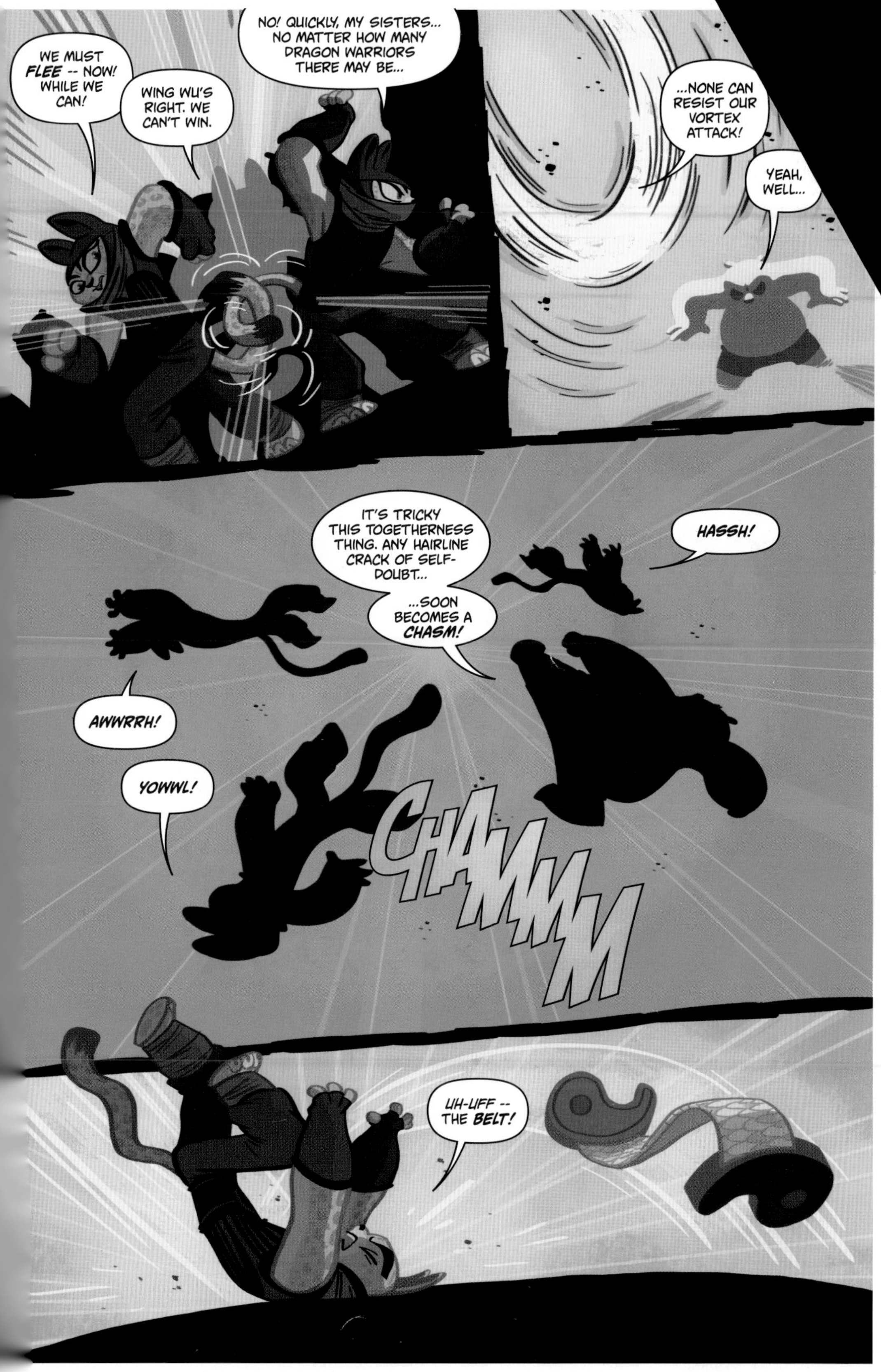
WE MUST FLEE -- NOW! WHILE WE CAN!
WING WU'S RIGHT. WE CAN'T WIN.
NO! QUICKLY, MY SISTERS... NO MATTER HOW MANY DRAGON WARRIORS THERE MAY BE...
...NONE CAN RESIST OUR VORTEX ATTACK!
YEAH, WELL...
IT'S TRICKY THIS TOGETHERNESS THING. ANY HAIRLINE CRACK OF SELF-DOUBT...
...SOON BECOMES A CHASM!
HASSH!
AWWRRH!
YOWWL!
CHAMMMM
UH-UFF -- THE BELT!

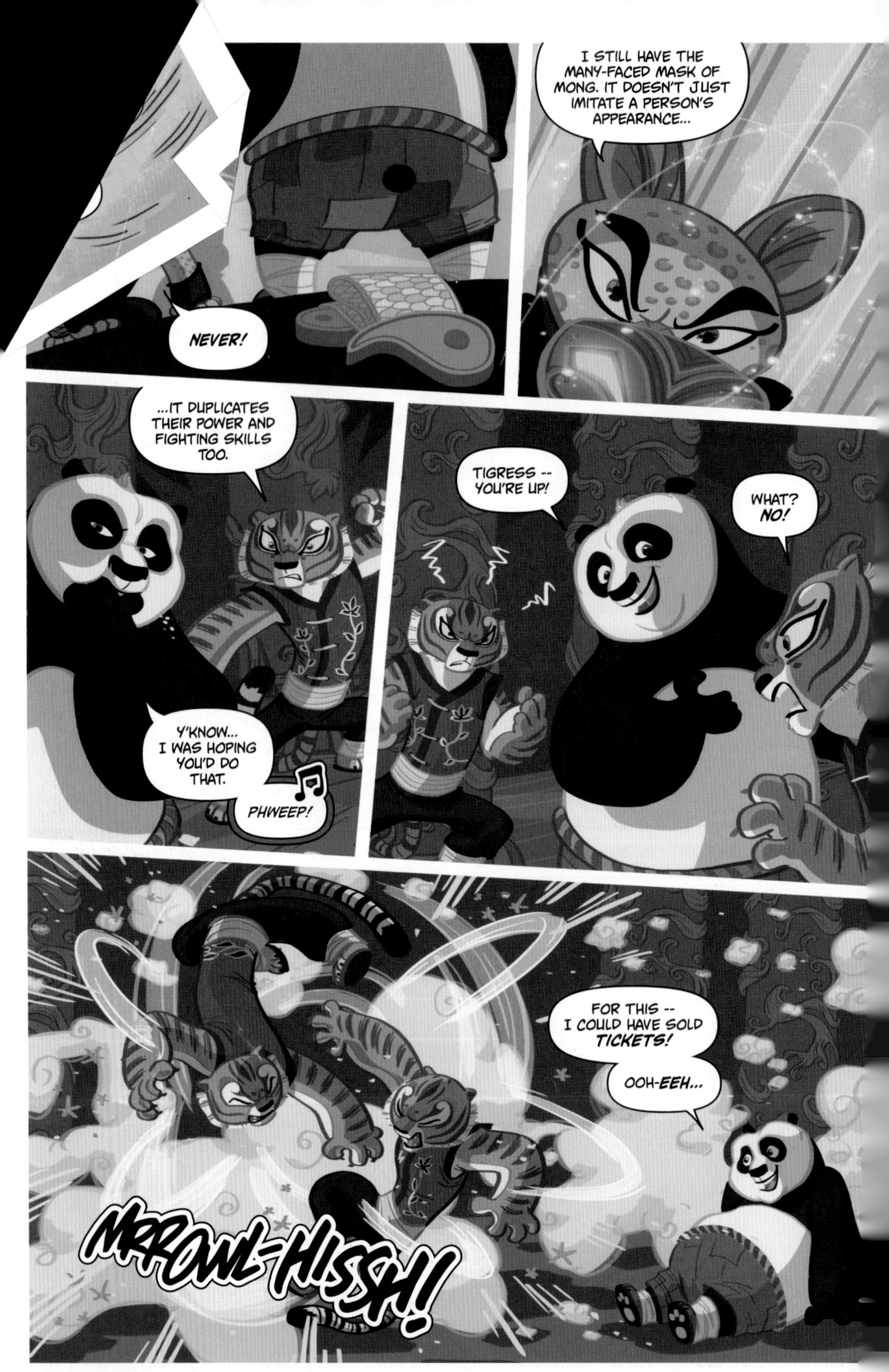

NEVER!
I STILL HAVE THE MANY-FACED MASK OF MONG. IT DOESN'T JUST IMITATE A PERSON'S APPEARANCE...
...IT DUPLICATES THEIR POWER AND FIGHTING SKILLS TOO.
Y'KNOW... I WAS HOPING YOU'D DO THAT.
PHWEEP!
TIGRESS -- YOU'RE UP!
WHAT? NO!
FOR THIS -- I COULD HAVE SOLD TICKETS!
OOH-EEH...
MRROWL-HISSH!

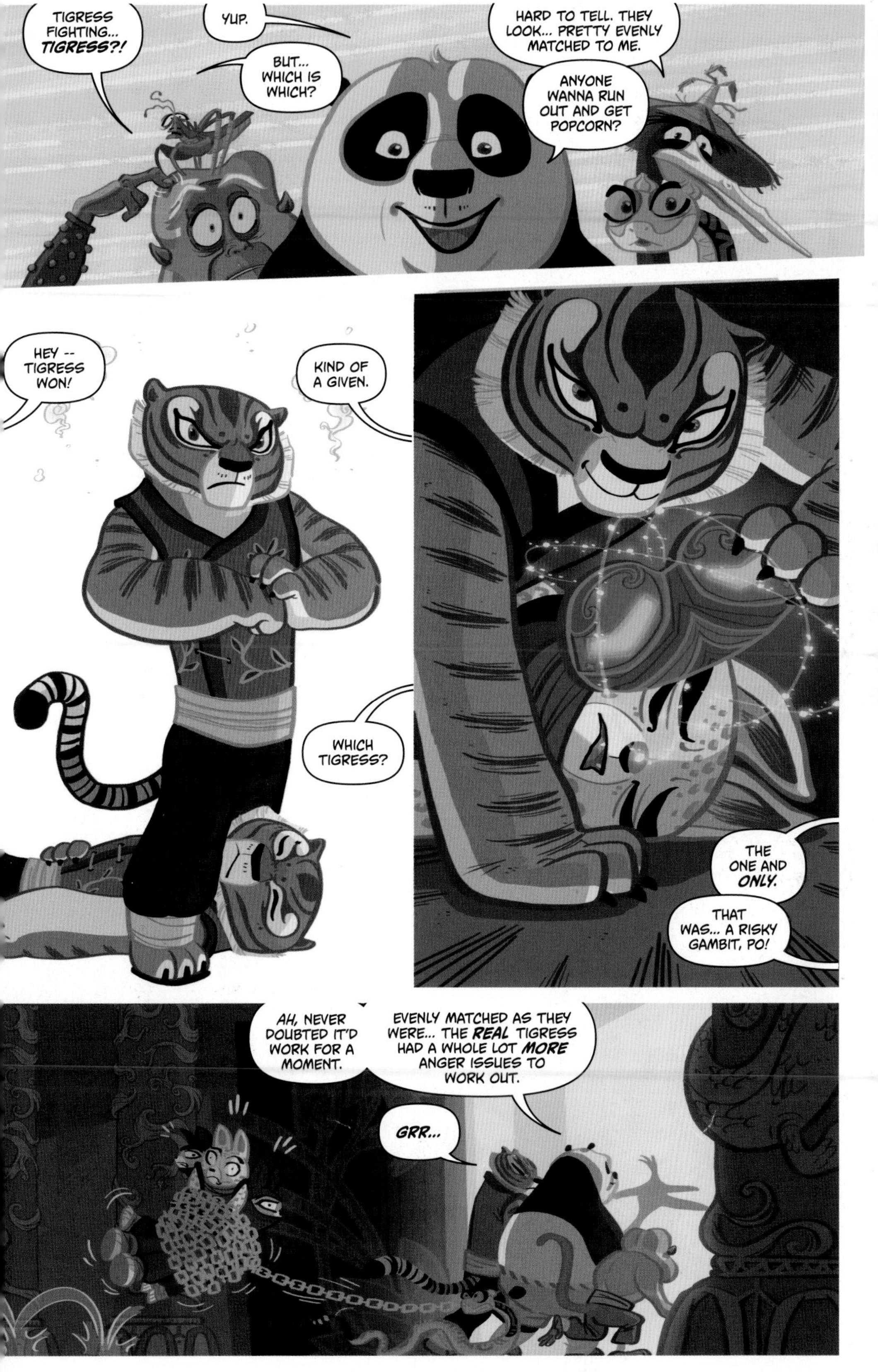
TIGRESS FIGHTING... TIGRESS?!
YUP.
BUT... WHICH IS WHICH?
HARD TO TELL. THEY LOOK... PRETTY EVENLY MATCHED TO ME.
ANYONE WANNA RUN OUT AND GET POPCORN?
HEY -- TIGRESS WON!
KIND OF A GIVEN.
WHICH TIGRESS?
THE ONE AND ONLY.
THAT WAS... A RISKY GAMBIT, PO!
AH, NEVER DOUBTED IT'D WORK FOR A MOMENT.
EVENLY MATCHED AS THEY WERE... THE REAL TIGRESS HAD A WHOLE LOT MORE ANGER ISSUES TO WORK OUT.
GRR...

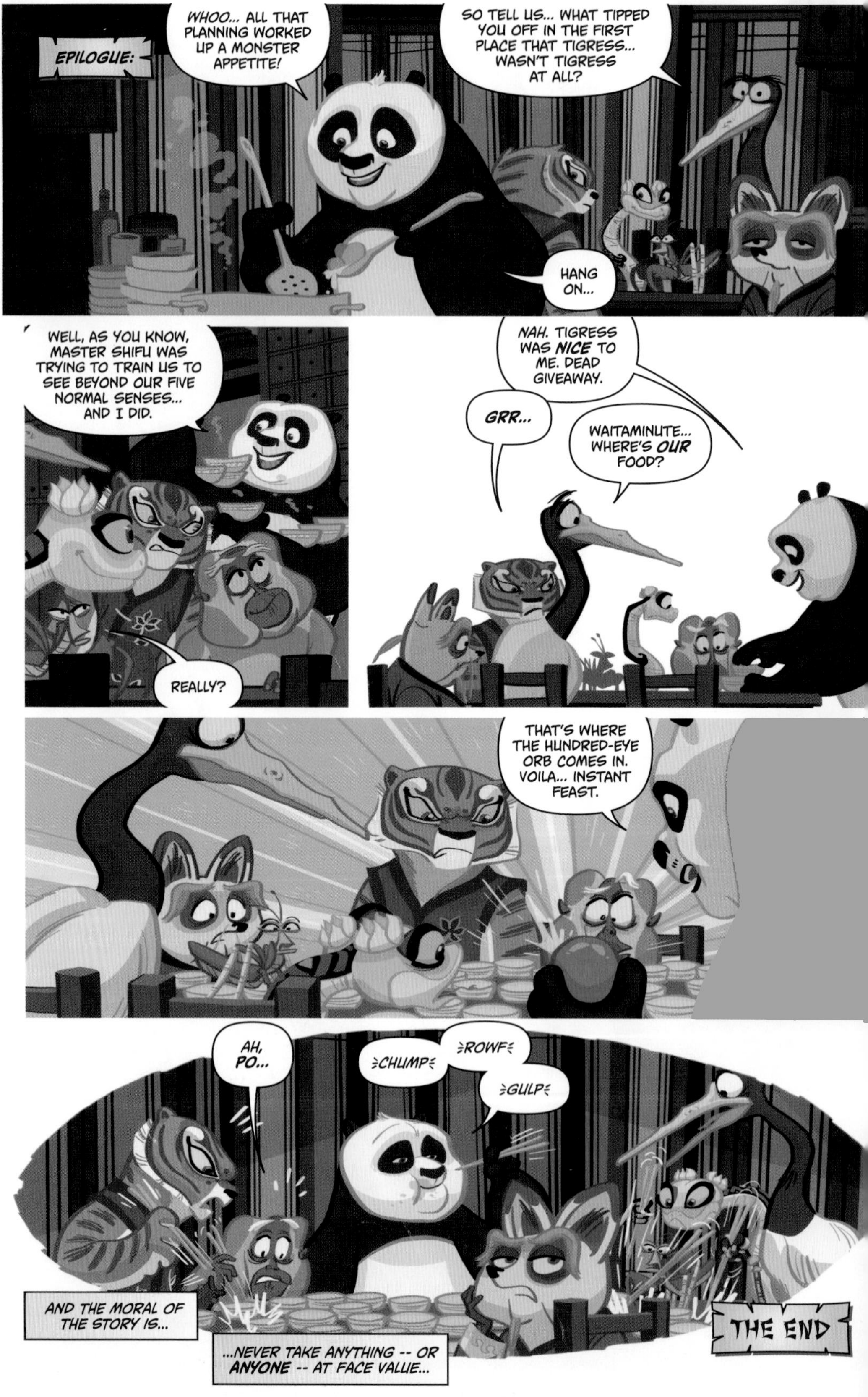
EPILOGUE:
WHOO... ALL THAT PLANNING WORKED UP A MONSTER APPETITE!
SO TELL US... WHAT TIPPED YOU OFF IN THE FIRST PLACE THAT TIGRESS... WASN'T TIGRESS AT ALL?
HANG ON...
WELL, AS YOU KNOW, MASTER SHIFU WAS TRYING TO TRAIN US TO SEE BEYOND OUR FIVE NORMAL SENSES... AND I DID.
REALLY?
NAH. TIGRESS WAS NICE TO ME. DEAD GIVEAWAY.
GRR...
WAITAMINUTE... WHERE'S OUR FOOD?
THAT'S WHERE THE HUNDRED-EYE ORB COMES IN. VOILA... INSTANT FEAST.
AH, PO...
CHUMP
ROWF
GULP
AND THE MORAL OF THE STORY IS...
...NEVER TAKE ANYTHING -- OR ANYONE -- AT FACE VALUE...
THE END

PO

NAME: Master Po

OTHER KNOWN ALIASES:
The Dragon Warrior

OCCUPATION: Dragon Warrior (and occasional Noodle Chef)

DAD: Mr Ping

KUNG FU TEACHER:
Master Shifu

FRIENDS: Tigress, Viper, Crane, Monkey and Mantis (AKA the Furious Five!)

BOSS: Master Shifu

COMBAT STYLE: Panda Style

FAMOUS VICTORIES: Tai Lung and Lord Shen

INTERESTS: Kung fu, dumplings, noodles

WARRIOR SELECTION

Initially, many believed Po was mistakenly chosen as the Dragon Warrior. He had an accident with some fireworks and was launched up into the air, landing right in front of the great Master Oogway as he selected the Dragon Warrior. Oogway's finger settled on Po! But Oogway knew it was fate.

BECOMING THE DRAGON WARRIOR

It was no easy task; it meant a lot of hard work, and a lot of bruises! One day, Master Shifu presented Po with the Dragon Scroll, which contained the secret to limitless power, and only the true Dragon Warrior could grasp its meaning. Po proved himself, understanding that the secret was to believe in yourself.

ORIGIN

Po's original village was attacked by a peacock named Lord Shen when he was just a baby. Po's mother and father sacrificed themselves to save Po, hiding him in a crate of radishes. Whilst Mr. Ping was surprised to discover Po in his radish order, he happily adopted him.

THE WU SISTERS

NAME: Su Wu, Wing Wu, Wan Wu
KNOWN AS: The Wu Sisters
SPECIES: Leopard
OCCUPATION: Criminals
DESIRED OCCUPATION: Rulers of China
LIVE: Prison/Wu Fortress, in Hubei Volcano (when they escape)
COMBAT STYLE: Dangerous
FAMOUS MOVES: Swirling Vortex (they lock their tails together and spin rapidly)
FAMILY: Su Wu, Wing Wu, Wan Wu...

FACTS FROM PRISON FILE

Many years ago, when these infamous villains were captured, they were all locked up in different prisons, for fear of how strong they are together. Su Wu was deemed so dangerous, she was put in a sarcophagus!

THE WU TO WATCH

Su Wu is the leader of the Wu Sisters. Together they are a force to be reckoned with, but Su is a ruthless fighter in her own right. She is extremely loyal to her sisters. She carries no qualms about hurting the innocent if they get in her way. Her great plan is to band together with all the other villains in China so they can rule over the entire country.

MR PING

NAME: Mr. Ping
SPECIES: Goose
FAMILY: Po (adopted son)
OCCUPATION: Noodle Chef
PLACE OF WORK: Dragon Warrior Tofu & Noodles (previously Mr. Ping's Noodle Shop)
HOBBIES: A master Chinese chess player (he even beat Master Shifu!)

SPECIAL ABILITIES

Much like Po, Mr. Ping can learn kung fu just from watching someone do a move once. He even taught himself the extremely difficult Chao Wa Punch Kick! Though he believes kung fu is nothing compared to noodles!

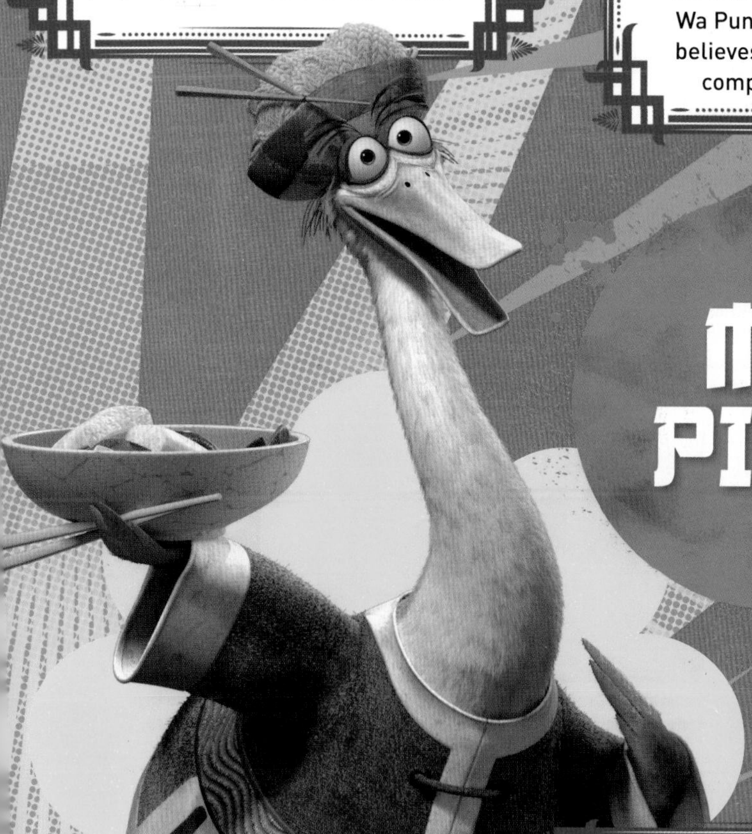

ORIGIN

Mr. Ping's father, and his father before him were noodle-makers. It was Mr. Ping's hope that Po would follow in his footsteps, but though he was disappointed, he couldn't help but be proud of his son being the Dragon Warrior.

FATHERLY ADVICE

Mr. Ping helped Po understand the secret to the Dragon Scroll, and thus become the Dragon Warrior, when he revealed the secret ingredient to his famous noodle soup, that it's nothing but your own belief that it's special.

DREAMWORKS DIGESTS
ALSO AVAILABLE

**Dreamworks
Classics, Volume 1**

**Home
Volume 1**

**Home
Volume 2**

**Kung Fu Panda, Vol 1
Coming Jan 12, 2016**

**Kung Fu Panda, Vol 2
Coming Jan 12, 2016**

**Penguins of
Madagascar, Vol 1**

**Penguins of
Madagascar, Vol 2**

**DreamWorks Dragons:
Riders of Berk, Vol 1**

**DreamWorks Dragons:
Riders of Berk, Vol 2**

**DreamWorks Dragons:
Riders of Berk, Vol 3**

**DreamWorks Dragons:
Riders of Berk, Vol 4**

**DreamWorks Dragons:
Riders of Berk, Vol 5**

**DreamWorks Dragons:
Riders of Berk, Vol 6**

**DreamWorks Dragons:
Defenders of Berk
Coming 22 March 2016**